From head to foot the figure was clad all in brass and seated on a chestnut warhorse draped with a canopy of russet silk. The gloves and the boots were of brass links stitched upon leather. The belt was of brass chain brought together by a huge brass buckle.

And then there was the face—the golden brown eyes, steady and stern, the heavy red moustache, the red eyebrows, the bronze tan.

It could be no other.

"Count Brass!" gasped Dorian Hawkmoon. "What are you? What brings you to the Kamarg?"

"My death. I am dead, am I not?"

"The Count Brass I knew is dead, slain at Londra more than five years since."

"You are the one called Hawkmoon of Köln?"

"I am Dorian Hawkmoon, Duke of Köln, aye."

"Then I must slay you, it seems."

MICHAEL MOORCOCK
COUNT BRASS

The Chronicles of Castle Brass
Volume I

ACE BOOKS, NEW YORK

You can join the Michael Moorcock fan club! Write to: *Nomads of the Time Streams:* The International Michael Moorcock Appreciation Society, PO Box 451048, Atlanta, GA 30345-1048.

This Ace book contains the complete
text of the original edition.
It has been completely reset in a typeface
designed for easy reading and was printed
from new film.

COUNT BRASS

An Ace Book / published by arrangement with
the author

PRINTING HISTORY
Previously published in Great Britain and the United States.
Dell edition / February 1981
Berkley edition / February 1985
Ace edition / June 1988

ISBN: 0-441-11775-9

Ace Books are published by The Berkley Publishing Group,
200 Madison Avenue, New York, New York 10016.
The name "ACE" and the "A" logo are
trademarks belonging to Charter Communications, Inc.

10   9   8   7   6   5   4   3   2   1

This book is for Bill Butler
and Harrods of Knightsbridge
for entirely opposite reasons.

Then the Earth grew old, its landscapes
mellowing and showing signs of age, its
ways becoming whimsical and strange in
the manner of a man in his last years.
　　　　　—The High History of the Runestaff

And when this History was done there
followed it another. A Romance involving
the same participants in experiences
perhaps even more bizarre and awesome
than the last. And again the ancient Castle
of Brass in the marshy Kamarg was the
centre for much of this action...
　　　　　—The Chronicles of Castle Brass

CONTENTS

BOOK ONE
OLD FRIENDS

BOOK TWO
OLD ENEMIES

BOOK THREE
OLD DREAMS AND NEW

EPILOGUE

book one

OLD FRIENDS

chapter one

THE HAUNTING OF DORIAN HAWKMOON

It had taken all these five years to restore the land of Kamarg, to repopulate its marshes with the giant scarlet flamingoes, the wild white bulls and the horned great horses which had once teemed here before the coming of the Dark Empire's bestial armies. It had taken all these five years to rebuild the watchtowers of the borders, to put up the towns and to erect tall Castle Brass in all its massive, masculine beauty. And, if anything, in these five years of peace, the walls were built stronger, the watchtowers taller, for, as Dorian Hawkmoon had said once to Queen Flana of Granbretan, the world was still wild and there was still little justice in it.

Dorian Hawkmoon, the Duke of Köln, and his bride, Yisselda, Countess of Brass, old, dead Count Brass's daughter, were the only two who remained of that group of heroes who had served the Runestaff against the Dark Empire and finally defeated Granbretan in the great Battle of Londra, putting Queen Flana, sad Queen Flana, upon the throne so that she might guide her cruel and decadent nation towards humanity and vitality.

Count Brass had died slaying three barons (Adaz Promp, Mygel Holst and Saka Gerden) and in turn was slain by a Spearman of the Order of the Goat.

Oladahn of the Bulgar Mountains, beastman and loyal friend of Hawkmoon, had been hacked to pieces by the war axes of the Order of the Pig.

Bowgentle, the unwarlike, the philosophical, had been savaged and decapitated by Pigs, Goats and Hounds to the number of twelve.

Huillam D'Averc, mocker of everything, whose only faith had seemed to be in his own lack of good health, who had loved and been loved by Queen Flana, had died most ironically, riding to his love and being slain by one of her soldiers who thought D'Averc attacked her.

Four heroes died. Thousands of other heroes, unnamed in the histories, but brave, also died in the service of the Runestaff, in the destruction of the Dark Empire tyranny.

And a great villain died. Baron Meliadus of Kroiden, most ambitious, most ambivalent, most awful of all the aristocrats of Granbretan, died upon the sword of Hawkmoon, died beneath the edge of the mystical Sword of the Dawn.

And the ruined world seemed free.

But that had been five years hence. Much has passed since then. Two children had been born to Hawkmoon and the Countess of Brass. They were called Manfred, who had red hair and his grandfather's voice and health and stood to be his grandfather's size and strength, and Yarmila, who had golden hair and her mother's gentle toughness of will, as well as her beauty. They were Brass stock, there was little in them of the Dukes of Köln, and perhaps that was why

Dorian Hawkmoon loved his children so fiercely and so well.

And beyond the walls of Castle Brass stood four statues to the four dead heroes, to remind the inhabitants of the castle of what they had fought for and at what cost. And Dorian Hawkmoon would often take his children to those statues and tell them of the Dark Empire and its deeds. And they were pleased to listen. And Manfred assured his father that when he grew up his deeds would be as great as those of old Count Brass, whom he so resembled.

And Hawkmoon would say that he hoped they would have no need of heroes when Manfred was grown.

Then, seeing disappointment in his son's face, he would laugh and say there were many kinds of heroes and if Manfred had his grandfather's wisdom and diplomacy, his strong sense of justice, that would make him the best kind of hero—a justice-maker. And Manfred would only be somewhat consoled, for there is little that is romantic about a judge and much that is attractive to a four-year-old boy about a warrior.

And sometimes Hawkmoon and Yisselda would take their children riding through the wild marshlands of the Kamarg, beneath wide skies of pastel colours, of faded reds and yellows, where the reeds were brown and dark green and orange and, in the appropriate season, bent before the mistral. And they would see a herd of white bulls thunder by, or a herd of horned horses. And they might see a flock of huge scarlet flamingoes suddenly take to the air and drift on broad wings over the heads of the invading human beings, not knowing that it was Dorian Hawkmoon's responsibility, as it had been that of Count Brass, to protect the wildlife of the Kamarg and never to kill it, and only sometimes to tame it to provide riding beasts for land and sky. Originally this had been why the great watchtowers had been built and why the men who occupied those watchtowers were called

Guardians. But now they guarded the human populace as well as the beasts, guarded them from any threat from beyond the Kamarg's borders (for no native-bred Karmargian would consider harming the animals which were found nowhere else in the world). The only beasts that were hunted (save for food) in the marshes were the baragoon, the marsh gibberers, the things which had once been men themselves before becoming the victims of sorcerous experiments conducted by an evil Lord Guardian who had been done away with by old Count Brass. But there were only one or two baragoons left in the Kamarg lands now for hunters had little difficulty identifying them—they were over eight feet tall, five feet broad, bile-coloured and they slithered on their bellies through the swamps, occasionally rising to rush upon whatever prey they could now find in the marshlands. None the less, on their rides, Yisselda and Dorian Hawkmoon would take care to avoid the places still thought to be inhabited by the baragoon.

Hawkmoon had come to love the Kamarg more than his own ancestral lands in far-off Germany, had even renounced his title to those lands now ruled well by an elected council as indeed were many of the European lands who had lost their hereditary rulers and chosen, since the defeat of the Dark Empire, to become republics.

Yet, for all that Hawkmoon was loved and respected by the people of the Kamarg, he was aware that he did not replace old Count Brass in their eyes. He could never do that. They sought Countess Yisselda's advice as often as they sought his and they looked with great favour on young Manfred, seeing him almost as a reincarnation of their old Lord Guardian.

Another man might have resented all this, but Hawkmoon, who had loved Count Brass as well as had they, accepted it with good grace. He had had enough of command, of heroics. He preferred to live the life of a simple country gentleman and wherever possible let the people have control of their own affairs. His ambitions were simple, too—to love his beautiful wife Yisselda and to ensure the happiness of his children. His days of history-making were over. All that he had left to remind him of his struggles against Granbretan was an oddly shaped scar in the centre of his forehead—where once had reposed the dreadful Black Jewel, the Braineater implanted there by Baron Kalan of Vitall when, years before, Hawkmoon had been recruited against his will to serve the Dark Empire against Count Brass. Now the jewel was gone and so was Baron Kalan, who had committed suicide after the Battle of Londra. A brilliant scientist, but perhaps the most warped of all the barons of Granbretan, Kalan had been unable to conceive of continuing to exist under the new and, in his view, soft order imposed by Queen Flana, who had succeeded the King Emperor Huon after Baron Meliadus had slain him in a desperate effort to make himself controller of Granbretan's policies.

Hawkmoon sometimes wondered what would have happened to Baron Kalan, or, for that matter, Taragorm, Master of the Palace of Time, who had perished when one of Kalan's fiendish weapons had exploded during the Battle of Londra, if they had lived on. Could they have been put into the service of Queen Flana and their talents used to rebuild the world they had helped destroy? Probably not, he thought. They were insane. Their characters had been wholly shaped by the perverted and insane philosophies which had led Granbretan to make war upon the world and come close to conquering it all.

After one of their marshland rides, the family would return to Aigues-Mortes, the walled and ancient town which was the principal city of the Kamarg, and to Castle Brass which stood on a hill in the very centre. Built of the same white stone as the majority of the town's houses, Castle

Brass was a mixture of architectural styles which, somehow, did not seem to clash with each other. Over the centuries there had been additions and renovations; at the whim of different owners parts had been torn down and other parts built. Most of the windows were of intricately detailed stained glass, though the window frames themselves were as often round as they were square and as square as they were oblong or oval. Turrets and towers sprang up from the main mass of stone in all kinds of surprising places; there were even one or two minarets in the manner of Arabian palaces. And Dorian Hawkmoon, following the fashion of his own German folk, had had many flagstaffs erected and upon these staffs floated beautiful coloured banners, including those of the Counts of Brass and the Dukes of Köln. Gargoyles festooned the gutters of the castle and many a gable was carved in stone in the likeness of a Kamargian beast—the bull, the flamingo, the horned horse and the marsh bear.

There was about Castle Brass, as there had been in the days of Count Brass himself, something at once impressive and comfortable. The castle had not been built to impress anyone with either the taste or the power of its inhabitants. It had hardly been built for strength (though it had already proven its strength) and aesthetic considerations, too, had not been made when rebuilding it. It had been built for comfort and this was a rare thing in a castle. It could be that it was the only castle in the world that had been built with such considerations in mind! Even the terraced gardens outside the castle walls had a homely appearance, growing vegetables and flowers of every sort, supplying not only the castle but much of the town with its basic requirements.

When they returned from their rides the family would sit down to a good, plain meal which would be shared with many of its retainers, then the children would be taken to bed by Yisselda and she would tell them a story. Sometimes the story would be an ancient one, from the time before the

Tragic Millennium, sometimes it would be one she would make up herself and sometimes, at the insistence of Manfred and Yarmila, Dorian Hawkmoon would be called for and he would tell them of some of his adventures in distant lands when he served the Runestaff. He would tell them of how he had met little Oladahn, whose body and face had been covered in fine, reddish hair, and who had claimed to be the kin of Mountain Giants. He would tell them of Amarehk beyond the great sea to the north and the magical city of Dnark where he had first seen the Runestaff itself. Admittedly, Hawkmoon had to modify these tales, for the truth was darker and more terrible than most adult minds could conceive. He spoke most often of his dead friends and their noblest deeds, keeping alive the memories of Count Brass, Bowgentle, D'Averc and Oladahn. Already these deeds were legendary throughout Europe.

And when the stories were done, Yisselda and Dorian Hawkmoon would sit in deep armchairs on either side of the great fireplace over which hung Count Brass's armour of brass and his broadsword, and they would talk or they would read.

From time to time they would receive letters from Londra, from Queen Flana telling how her policies progressed. Londra, that insane roofed city, had been almost entirely dismantled and fine, open buildings put up instead on both sides of the River Tayme, which no longer ran blood red. The wearing of masks had been abolished and most of the people of Granbretan had, after a while, become used to revealing their naked faces, though some die-hards had had to receive mild punishment for their insistence on clinging to the old, mad ways of the Dark Empire. The Orders of the Beasts had also been outlawed and people had been encouraged to leave the darkness of their cities and return to the all but deserted and overgrown countryside of Granbretan, where vast forests of oak, elm or pine stretched for

miles. For centuries Granbretan had lived on plunder and
now she had to feed herself. Therefore the soldiers who had
belonged to the beast orders were put to farming, to clearing
the forests, to raising herds and planting crops. Local coun-
cils were set up to represent the interests of the people.
Queen Flana had called a parliament and this parliament
now advised her and helped her rule justly. It was strange
how swiftly a warlike nation, a nation of military castes,
had been encouraged to become a nation of farmers and
foresters. The majority of the people of Granbretan had
taken to their new lives with relief once it dawned on them
that they were now free of the madness that had once in-
fected the whole land—and sought, indeed, to infect the
world.

And so the quiet days passed at Castle Brass.

And so they would have passed for always (until Manfred
and Yarmila grew up and Hawkmoon and Yisselda became
middle-aged and, eventually, old in their contentment, dying
peacefully and cheerfully, knowing that the Kamarg was
secure and that the days of the Dark Empire could never
return) but for something strange that began to happen towards the close of the sixth summer since the Battle of
Londra when, to his astonishment, Dorian Hawkmoon found
that the people of Aigues-Mortes were beginning to offer
him peculiar looks when he hailed them in the streets—
some refusing to acknowledge him at all and others scowling
and muttering and turning aside as he approached.

It was Dorian Hawkmoon's habit, as it had been Count
Brass's, to attend the great celebrations marking the end of
the summer's work. Then Aigues-Mortes would be decorated with flowers and banners and the citizens would put
on their most elaborate finery, young white bulls would be
allowed to charge at will through the streets and the guardians of the watchtowers would ride about in their polished
armour and silk surcoats, their flame-lances on their hips.

And there would be bull contests in the immeasurably ancient amphitheatre on the outskirts of the town. Here was where Count Brass had once saved the life of the great toreador Mahtan Just when he was being gored to death by a gigantic bull. Count Brass had leaped into the ring and wrestled the bull with his bare hands, bringing the beast to its knees and winning the acclaim of the crowd, for Count Brass had then been well into middle age.

But nowadays the festival was not a purely local affair. Ambassadors from all over Europe would come to honour the surviving hero and heroine of Londra and Queen Flana herself had visited Castle Brass on two previous occasions. This year, however, Queen Flana had been kept at home by affairs of state and one of her nobles attended in her name. Hawkmoon was pleased to note that Count Brass's dream of a unified Europe was beginning to become reality. The wars with Granbretan had helped break down the old boundaries and had brought the survivors together in a common cause. Europe still consisted of about a thousand small provinces, each independent of any other, but they worked in concert on many projects concerning the general good.

The ambassadors came from Scandia, from Muscovy, from Arabia, from the lands of the Greeks and the Bulgars, from Ukrainia, from Nürnberg and Catalania. They came in carriages, on horseback or in ornithopters whose design was borrowed from Granbretan. And they brought gifts and they brought speeches (some long and some short) and they spoke of Dorian Hawkmoon as if he were a demigod.

In past years their praise had found enthusiastic response in the people of the Kamarg. But for some reason this year their speeches did not get quite the same quality of applause as they once had. Few, however, noticed. Only Hawkmoon and Yisselda noticed and, without being resentful, they were deeply puzzled.

The most fulsome of all the speeches made in the ancient

bullring of Aigues-Mortes came from Lonson, Prince of
Shkarlan, cousin to Queen Flana, ambassador from Granbretan. Lonson was young and an enthusiastic supporter of
the queen's policies. He had been barely seventeen when
the Battle of Londra had robbed his nation of its evil power
and thus he bore no great resentment of Dorian Hawkmoon
von Köln—indeed, he saw Hawkmoon as a saviour, who
had brought peace and sanity to his island kingdom. Prince
Lonson's speech was rich with admiration for the new Lord
Protector of the Kamarg. He recalled great deeds of battle,
great achievements of will and self-discipline, great cunning
in the arts of strategy and diplomacy by which, he said,
future generations would remember Dorian Hawkmoon. Not
only had Hawkmoon saved continental Europe—he had
saved the Dark Empire from itself.

Seated in his traditional box with all his foreign guests
about him, Dorian Hawkmoon listened to the speech with
embarrassment and hoped it would soon end. He was dressed
in ceremonial armour which was as ornate as it was uncomfortable and the back of his neck itched horribly. While
Prince Lonson spoke it would not be polite to remove the
helmet and scratch. He looked at the crowd seated on the
granite benches of the amphitheatre and seated on the ground
of the ring itself. Whereas most of the people were listening
with approval to Prince Lonson's speech, others were muttering to each other, scowling. One old man, whom Hawkmoon recognised as an ex-guardian who had fought beside
Count Brass in many of his battles, even spat into the dust
of the arena when Prince Lonson spoke of Dorian Hawkmoon's unswerving loyalty to his comrades.

Yisselda also noticed this and she frowned, glancing at
Hawkmoon to see if he had noticed. Their eyes met. Dorian
Hawkmoon shrugged and gave her a little smile. She smiled
back, but the frown did not altogether leave her brow.

And at last the speech was over and applauded and the

people began to leave the arena so that the first of the bulls might be driven in and the first toreador attempt to remove the colourful ribbons which were tied to the beast's horns (for it was not the custom of the folk of the Kamarg to exhibit their courage by slaying animals—instead skill alone was pitted against the snorting savagery of the very fiercest bulls).

But when the crowd had departed there was one who remained. Now Hawkmoon recalled his name. It was Czernik, originally a Bulgar mercenary who had thrown in his lot with Count Brass and ridden with him through a dozen campaigns. Czernik's face was flushed, as if he had been drinking, and his stance was unsteady as he pointed a finger up at Hawkmoon's box and spat again.

"Loyalty!" the old man croaked. "I know otherwise. I know who is Count Brass's murderer—who betrayed him to his enemies! Coward! Play-actor! False hero!"

Hawkmoon was stunned as he listened to Czernik rant. What could the old man mean?

Stewards ran into the ring to grasp Czernik's arms and attempt to hurry him off. But he struggled with them.

"Thus your master tries to silence the truth!" screamed Czernik. "But it cannot be silenced! He has been accused by the only one whose word can be trusted!"

If it had only been Czernik who had shown such animosity, Hawkmoon would have dismissed his ravings as senile. But Czernik was not the only one. Czernik had expressed what Hawkmoon had seen on more than a score of faces that day—and on previous days.

"Let him be!" Hawkmoon called, standing up and leaning forward over the balustrade. "Let him speak!"

For a moment the stewards were at a loss to know what to do. Then, reluctantly, they released the old man. Czernik stood there trembling, glaring into Hawkmoon's eyes.

"Now," Hawkmoon called. "Tell me of what you accuse me, Czernik. I will listen."

The attention of the whole populace of Aigues-Mortes was upon Hawkmoon and Czernik now. There was a stillness, a silence in the air.

Yisselda tugged at her husband's surcoat. "Do not listen to him, Dorian. He is drunk. He is mad."

"Tell me!" Hawkmoon demanded.

Czernik scratched his head of grey, thinning hair. He stared around him at the crowd. He mumbled something.

"Speak more clearly!" Hawkmoon said. "I am eager to hear, Czernik."

"I called you murderer and murderer you be!" Czernik said.

"Who told you that I am a murderer!"

Again Czernik's mumble was inaudible.

"Who told you?"

"The one you murdered!" Czernik screamed. "The one you betrayed."

"A dead man? Whom did I betray?"

"The one we all love. The one I followed across a hundred provinces. The one who saved my life twice. The one to whom, living or dead, I would ever give my loyalty."

Yisselda's whisper from behind Hawkmoon was incredulous. "He can speak of none other but my father..."

"Do you mean Count Brass?" Hawkmoon called.

"Aye!" cried Czernik defiantly. "Count Brass, who came to the Kamarg all those years ago and saved it from tyranny. Who fought the Dark Empire and saved the whole world! His deeds are well known. What was not known was that at Londra he was betrayed by one who not only coveted his daughter but coveted his castle, too. And killed him for them!"

"You lie," and Hawkmoon evenly. "If you were younger, Czernik, I would challenge you to defend your foul words with a sword. How could you believe such lies?"

"Many believe them!" Czernik gestured to indicate the

crowd. "Many here have heard what I have heard."

"*Where* have you heard this?" Yisselda joined her husband at the balustrade.

"In the marshlands beyond the town. At night. Some, like me, journeying home from another town—they have heard it."

"And from whose lying lips?" Hawkmoon was trembling with anger. He and Count Brass had fought side by side, each had been prepared to die for the other—and now this dreadful lie was being told—a lie which insulted Count Brass's memory. And that was why Hawkmoon was angry.

"From his own! From Count Brass's lips."

"Drunken fool! Count Brass is dead. You said as much yourself."

"Aye—but his ghost has returned to the Kamarg. Riding upon the back of his great horned horse in all his armour of gleaming brass, with his hair and his moustache all red as brass and his eyes like burnished brass. He is out there, treacherous Hawkmoon, in the marsh. He haunts you. And those who meet him are told of your treachery, how you deserted him when his enemies beset him, how you let him die in Londra."

"It *is* a lie!" shouted Yisselda. "I was there. I fought at Londra. Nothing could save my father."

"And," continued Czernik, his voice deepening but still loud, "I heard from Count Brass how you joined with your lover to deceive him."

"Oh!" Yisselda clapped her hands to her ears. "This is obscene! Obscene!"

"Be silent now, Czernik," warned Hawkmoon hollowly. "Still your tongue, for you go too far!"

"He awaits you in the marshes. He will take his vengeance upon you out there at night when next you travel beyond the walls of Aigues-Mortes—if you dare. And his ghost is still more of a hero, more of a man than are you, turncoat. Aye—turncoat you be. First you served Köln, then you served the Empire, then you turned against the Empire, then you aided the Empire in its plot against Count Brass, then once again you betrayed the Empire. Your history speaks for the truth of what I say. I am not mad. I am not drunk. There are others who have seen and heard what I have seen and heard."

"Then you have been deceived," said Yisselda firmly.

"It is you who have been deceived, my lady!" Czernik growled.

And then the stewards came forward again and Hawkmoon did not try to stop them as they dragged the old man from the amphitheatre.

The rest of the proceedings did not go well, after that. Hawkmoon's guests were too embarrassed to comment on the incident and the crowd's interest was not on the bulls or the toreadors who leaped so skilfully the ring, plucking the ribbons from the horns.

A banquet followed at Castle Brass. To the banquet had been invited all the local dignitaries of the Kamarg, as well as the ambassadors, and it was noticeable that four or five of the local people had not come. Hawkmoon ate little and drank more than was normal for him. He tried hard to rid himself of the gloomy mood into which Czernik's peculiar declarations had put him, but he found it difficult to smile even when his own children came down to greet him and be introduced to his guests. Every sentence he spoke required an effort and there was no flow of conversation, even among the guests. Many of the ambassadors made excuses and went early to their beds. And soon only Hawkmoon and Yisselda were left in the banqueting hall, still seated in their places at the head of the table, watching the servants clear away the remains of the meal.

"What could he have seen?" said Yisselda as, at last, the

servants, too, left. "What could he have heard Dorian?"

Hawkmoon shrugged. "He told us. Your father's ghost . . ."

"A baragoon more articulate than most?"

"He described your father. His horse. His armour. His face."

"But he was drunk even today."

"He said that others saw Count Brass and heard the same story from his lips."

"Then it is a plot. Some enemy of yours—one of the Dark Empire lords who survived unrepentant—dressed up with false whiskers and his face painted to resemble my father's."

"That could be," said Hawkmoon. "But would not Czernik of all people have seen through such a deception? He knew Count Brass for years."

"Aye. And knew him well," Yisselda admitted.

Hawkmoon rose slowly from his chair and walked heavily towards the fireplace where Count Brass's wargear hung. He looked up at it, reached out to finger it. He shook his head. "I must discover for myself what this 'ghost' is. Why should anyone seek to discredit me in this way? Who could my enemy be?"

"Czernik himself? Could he resent your presence at Castle Brass?"

"Czernik is old—near senile. He could not have invented such an elaborate deception."

"Has he not wondered why Count Brass should remain in the marshes complaining about me? That is not like Count Brass. He would come to his own castle if he were here. If he had a grudge he would tax me with it."

"You speak as if you believe Czernik now."

Hawkmoon sighed. "I must know more. I must find Czernik and question him . . ."

"I will send one of our retainers into the town."

"No. I will go into the town and search him out."

"Are you sure . . . ?"

"It is what I must do." He kissed her. "I'll put an end to this tonight. Why should we be plagued by phantoms we have not even seen?"

He wrapped a thick cloak of dark blue silk about his shoulders and kissed Yisselda once more before going out into the courtyard and ordering his horned horse saddled and harnessed. Some minutes later he rode out from the castle and down the winding road to the town. Few lights burned in Aigues-Mortes, for all that there was supposed to be a festival in the town. Evidently the townspeople had been as affected by the scene in the bullring as had Hawk-moon and his guests. The wind was beginning to blow as Hawkmoon reached the streets; the harsh mistral wind of the Kamarg, which the people hereabouts called the Life Wind, for it was supposed to have saved their land during the Tragic Millennium.

If Czernik was to be found anywhere it was in one of the taverns on the north side of town. Hawkmoon rode to the district, letting his horse make its own speed, for in many ways he was reluctant to repeat the earlier scene. He did not want to hear Czernik's lies again; they were lies which dishonoured all, even Count Brass, whom Czernik claimed to love.

The old taverns on the north side were primarily of wood, with only their foundations being made of the white stone of the Kamarg. The wood was painted in many different colours and some of the most ambitious of the taverns had even painted whole scenes across the frontages—several of the scenes commemorating the deeds of Hawkmoon himself and others recalling earlier exploits of Count Brass before he came to save the Kamarg, for Count Brass had fought (and often been a prime mover) in almost every famous battle of his day. Indeed, not a few of the taverns were named for Count Brass's battles, as well as those of the four heroes who had served the Runestaff. One tavern was called The Magyarian Campaign while another proclaimed itself The Battle of Cannes. Here were The Fort at Balancia, Nine Left Standing and The Banner Dipped in Blood—all recalling Count Brass's exploits. Czernik, if he had not fallen on his face in some gutter by now, would be bound to be in one of them.

Hawkmoon entered the nearest door, that of The Red Amulet (named for that mystic jewel he had once worn around his own neck), and found the place packed with old soldiers, many of whom he recognised. They were all pretty drunk, with big mugs of wine and ale in their hands. There was hardly a man among them who did not have scars on his face or limbs. Their laughter was harsh but not noisy— only their singing was loud. Hawkmoon felt pleased to be in such company and greeted many whom he knew. He went up to a one-armed Slavian—another of Count Brass's men—and greeted him with genuine pleasure.

"Josef Vedla! Good evening, Captain. How goes it with you?"

Vedla blinked and tried to smile. "A good evening to you, my lord. We have not seen you in our taverns for many a month." He lowered his eyes and took an interest in the contents of his wine-cup.

"Will you join me in a skin of the new wine?" Hawkmoon asked. "I hear it is singularly good this year. Perhaps some of our other old friends will—?"

"No thanks, my lord." Vedla rose. "I've had too much as it is." Awkwardly he pulled his cloak around him with his single hand.

Hawkmoon spoke directly. "Josef Vedla. Do you believe Czernik's tale of meeting Count Brass in the marsh?"

"I must go." Vedla walked towards the low doorway.

"Captain Vedla. Stop."

Reluctantly, Vedla stopped and slowly he turned to look at Hawkmoon.

"Do you believe that Count Brass told him I betrayed our cause? That I led Count Brass himself into a trap?"

Vedla scowled. "Czernik alone I would not believe. He grows old and remembers only his youth when he rode with Count Brass. Maybe I wouldn't believe any veteran, no matter what he told me—for we all still mourn for Court Brass and would have him come back to us."

"As would I."

Vedla sighed. "I believe you, my lord. Though few would, these days. At least—most are simply not sure..."

"Who else has seen this ghost?"

"Several merchants, journeying back late at night through the marsh roads. A young bull-catcher. Even one guardian on duty in an eastern tower claims to have seen the figure in the distance. A figure that was unmistakably Count Brass."

"Do you know where Czernik is now?"

"Probably in The Dnieper Crossing at the end of this alley. That's where he spends his pension these days."

They went out into the cobbled street.

Hawkmoon said: "Captian Vedla, can you believe that I would betray Count Brass?"

Vedla rubbed his pitted nose. "No. Nor can most. It is hard to think of you as a traitor, Duke of Köln. But the stories are so consistent. Everyone who has met this—this ghost—tells the same tale."

"But Count Brass—alive or dead—is not one to hover on the edges of the town complaining. If he wanted—if he wanted vengeance on me, do you not think he would come and claim it?"

"Aye. Count Brass was not a man to be indecisive. Yet,"

Captain Vedla smiled wanly, "we also know that ghosts are supposed to act according to the customs of ghosts."

"You believe in ghosts, then?"

"I believe in nothing. I believe in everything. This world has taught me that lesson. What of the events concerning the Runestaff—would an ordinary man believe that they really took place?"

Hawkmoon could not help but return Vedla's smile. "I take your point. Well, good night to you, Captain."

"Good night, my lord."

Josef Vedla strode off in the opposite direction while Hawkmoon led his horse down the street to where he could see the sign of the tavern called The Dnieper Crossing. The paint was peeling on the sign and the tavern itself sagged as if one of its central beams had been removed. It looked an unsavoury place and the smell which came out of it was a mixture of sour wine, animal dung, grease and vomit. It was evident why a drunkard would choose it, for more oblivion could be bought here at the cheapest price.

The place was almost empty as Hawkmoon ducked his head through the door and went inside. A few brands and candles illuminated the room. The unclean floor and the filthy benches and tables, the cracked leather of the wine-skins strewn here and there, the chipped wooden and clay beakers, the ill-clothed men and women who sat hunched or lay sprawled in corners, all gave credence to Hawkmoon's original impression. People did not come to The Dnieper Crossing for social reasons. They came here to get drunk as quickly as was possible.

A small, dirty man with a fringe of black, greasy hair around his bald pate, slid from a patch of darkness and smiled up at Hawkmoon. "Ale, my lord? Good wine?"

"Czernik," said Hawkmoon. "Is he here?"

"Aye." The small man jerked a thumb towards the corner

and a door marked Privy. "He's in there making space for
more. He'll be out shortly. Shall I call him?"

"No." Hawkmoon looked around and then sat down on
a bench he judged to be somewhat cleaner than the rest.
"I'll wait for him."

"And a cup of wine while you wait?"

"Very well."

Hawkmoon left the wine untouched as he waited for
Czernik to emerge. At last the old veteran came stumbling
out and went straight to the bar. "Another flagon," he mumbled. He patted at his clothes, looking for his purse. He had
not seen Hawkmoon.

Hawkmoon rose. "Czernik?"

Czernik whirled around and almost fell over. He fumbled
for a sword he had long since pawned to buy more drink.
"Have you come to kill me, traitor?" His bleary eyes slowly
sharpened with hatred and fear. "Must I die for telling the
truth. If Count Brass were here . . . You know what this place
is called?"

"The Dnieper Crossing."

"Aye. We fought side by side, Count Brass and I, at The
Dnieper Crossing. Against Prince Ruchtof's armies, against
his cossaki. And the river was dammed with their bodies
so that its course was changed for all time. And at the end
of it all Prince Ruchtof's armies were dead and Count Brass
and I were the only two of our side left alive."

"I know the tale."

"Then know that I am brave. That I do not fear you. Kill
me, if you wish. But you shall not silence Count Brass
himself."

"I did not come to silence you, Czernik, but to listen.
Tell me again what you saw and what you heard."

Czernik glared suspiciously at Hawkmoon. "I told you
this afternoon."

"I wish to hear it once more. Without any of your own

accusations. Tell me, as you remember them, Count Brass's words to you."

Czernik shrugged. "He said that you had coveted his lands and his daughter ever since you first came to the Kamarg. He said that you had proved yourself a traitor several times over before you ever met him. He said that you fought the Dark Empire at Köln, then joined with the Beast Lords, even though they had slain your own father. Then you turned against the Empire when you thought you were strong enough, but they defeated you and took you back in chains of gilded iron to Londra where, in exchange for your own life you agreed to help them in a plot to betray Count Brass. Once out of their hands you came to the Kamarg and thought it easier to betray your Empire masters once again. This you did. Then you used your friends— Count Brass, Oladahn, Bowgentle and D'Averc—to beat the Empire and when they were no longer useful to you, you arranged things so that they should die in the Battle of Londra."

"A convincing story," said Hawkmoon grimly. "It fits the facts well enough, though it leaves out details which would vindicate my actions. A clever fabrication, indeed."

"You say Count Brass lies?"

"I say that what you saw in the marshes—the ghost or mortal—is not Count Brass. I know I speak the truth, Czernik, for I have no betrayals on my conscience. Count Brass knew the truth. Why should he lie after death?"

"I know Count Brass and I know you. I know that Count Brass would not tell such a lie. In diplomacy he was cunning—we all know that. But to his friends he spoke only the truth."

"Then what you saw was not Count Brass."

"What I saw was Count Brass. His ghost. Count Brass as he was when I rode at his side holding his banner for him when we went against the League of Eight to Italia,

two years before we came to the Kamarg. I know Count
Brass . . ."

Hawkmoon frowned. "And what was his message?"

"He waits for you in the marshes every night, there to
take his vengeance upon you."

Hawkmoon drew a deep breath. He adjusted his sword-
belt on his hip. "Then I will go to him tonight."

Czernik looked curiously at Hawkmoon. "You are not
afraid?"

"I am not. I know that whoever you saw cannot be Count
Brass. Why should I fear a fraud?"

"Perhaps you do not remember betraying him?" Czernik
suggested vaguely. "Perhaps it was all done by the jewel
you once wore in your forehead? Could it be the jewel which
forced you to such actions, so that when it was removed
you forgot all that you had planned?"

Hawkmoon offered Czernik a bleak smile. "I thank you
for that, Czernik. But I doubt if the jewel controlled me to
that extent. Its nature was somewhat different." He frowned.
For a moment he had begun to wonder if Czernik were
right. It would be horrifying if it were true . . . But no, it
could not be true. Yisselda would have known the truth,
however much he might have tried to hide it. Yisselda knew
he was no traitor.

Yet something was haunting the marshlands and trying
to turn the folk of the Kamarg against him and therefore he
must get to grips with it once and for all—lay the ghost
and prove to people like Czernik that he had betrayed no
one.

He said nothing more to Czernik but turned and strode
from the tavern, mounting his heavy black stallion and turning its head towards the town gates.

Through the gates he went and out into the moonlit marsh,
hearing the first distant, keening notes of the mistral, feeling
its cold breath on his cheek, seeing the surface of the lagoons

ripple and the reeds perform an agitated dance in anticipation of the wind's full force which would come a few days later.

Again he let his horse find its own route, for it knew the marsh better than did he. And meanwhile he peered through the gloom, looking this way and that; looking for a ghost.

chapter two

THE MEETING IN THE MARSH

The marsh was full of small sounds—scuttlings and slitherings, coughs, barks and hoots as the night animals went about their business. Sometimes a larger beast would emerge from the darkness and blunder past Hawkmoon. Sometimes there would be a heavy splash from a lagoon as a large fish-eating owl plunged upon its prey. But no human figure—ghost or mortal—was seen by the Duke of Köln as he rode deeper and deeper into the darkness.

Dorian Hawkmoon was confused. He was bitter. He had looked forward to a life of rural tranquillity. The only problems he had anticipated were the problems of breeding and planting, of the ordinary business of raising children.

And now this damned mystery had emerged. Not even a threat of war would have disturbed him half as much. War, albeit with the Dark Empire, was clean compared to this. If he had seen the brazen ornithopters of Granbretan in the skies, if he had seen beast-masked armies and grotesque carriages and all the other bizarre paraphernalia of the Dark Empire in the distance, he would have known how to deal with it. Or if the Runestaff had called him, he would have known how to respond.

But this was insidious. How could he cope with rumours, with ghosts, with old friends being turned against him?

Still the horned stallion plodded on through the marsh paths. Still there was no sign that the marsh was occupied by anyone other than Hawkmoon himself. He began to feel tired, for he had risen much earlier than usual in order to prepare himself for the festival. He began to suspect that there was nothing out here, that Czernik and the others had imagined it all, after all. He smiled to himself. He had been a fool to take a drunkard's ravings seriously.

And, of course, it was at that moment that it appeared to him. It was seated on a hornless chestnut warhorse and the warhorse was draped with a canopy of russet silk. The armour shone in the moonlight and it was all of heavy brass. Burnished brass helmet, very plain and practical; burnished brass breastplate and greaves. From head to foot the figure was clad in brass. The gloves and the boots were of brass links stitched upon leather. The belt was of brass chain brought together by a huge brass buckle and the belt supported a brass scabbard. In the scabbard rested something which was not of brass but of good steel. A broadsword. And then there was the face— the golden brown eyes, steady and stern, the heavy red moustache, the red eyebrows, the bronze tan.

It could be no other.

"Count Brass!" gasped Hawkmoon. And then he closed his mouth and studied the figure, for he had seen Count Brass dead on the battlefield.

There was something different about this man and it did not take Hawkmoon more than a moment to realize that Czernik had spoken the literal truth when he said it was the same Count Brass beside whom he had fought at the Dnieper

Crossing. This Count Brass was at least twenty years younger than the one whom Hawkmoon had first met when he visited the Kamarg seven or eight years previously.

The eyes flickered and the great head, seemingly all of brazen metal, turned slightly so that those eyes now peered directly into Hawkmoon's.

"Are you the one?" said the deep voice of Count Brass. "My nemesis?"

"Nemesis?" Hawkmoon uttered a sharp laugh. "I thought you had to be mine, Count Brass!"

"I am confused." The voice was definitely the voice of Count Brass, but it had a slightly dreamy quality to it. And Count Brass's eyes did not focus with their old, familiar clarity upon Hawkmoon's.

"What are you?" Hawkmoon demanded. "What brings you to the Kamarg?"

"My death. I am dead, am I not?"

"The Count Brass whom I knew is dead. He died at Londra more than five years since. I hear that I have been accused of that death."

"You are the one called Hawkmoon of Köln?"

"I am Dorian Hawkmoon, Duke of Köln, aye."

"Then I must slay you, it seems." This Count Brass spoke with some reluctance.

For all that his head whirled, Hawkmoon could see that Count Brass (or whatever the creature was) was quite as uncertain of himself as was Hawkmoon at that moment. For one thing, while Hawkmoon had recognized Count Brass, this man had not recognized Hawkmoon.

"Why must you slay me? Who told you to slay me?"

"The oracle. Though I am dead now, I may live again. But if I live again I must ensure that I do not die at the Battle of Londra. Therefore I must kill the one who would lead me to that battle and betray me to those against whom

I fight. That one is Dorian Hawkmoon of Köln, who covets my land and—and my daughter."

"I have lands of my own and your daughter was betrothed to me before the Battle of Londra. Someone deceives you, friend ghost."

"Why should the oracle deceive me?"

"Because there are such things as false oracles. Where do you come from?"

"From? Why, from Earth?"

"Where do you believe this place to be, in that case?"

"The netherworld, of course. A place from which few escape. But I can escape. Only I must slay you first, Dorian Hawkmoon."

"Something seeks to destroy me through you, Count Brass—if Count Brass you be. I cannot begin to explain this mystery, but I believe that you think you really are Count Brass and that I am your enemy. Perhaps all is a lie—perhaps only part."

A frown passed across the Count's brazen brow. "You confuse me. I do not understand. I was not warned of this."

Hawkmoon's lips were dry. He was so bewildered that he could barely think. So many emotions moved in him at the same time. There was grief for the memory of his dead friend. There was hatred for whoever it was sought to mock that memory. There was fear in case this should be a ghost. There was sympathy, should this really be Count Brass raised from the dead and turned into an automaton.

He began to suspect not the Runestaff now, but the science of the Dark Empire. This whole affair had the stamp of the perverse genius of the scientists of Granbretan. But how could they have affected it? The two great sorcerer-scientists of the Dark Empire, Taragorm and Kalan, were dead. There had been none to equal them while they lived, and none to replace them when they died.

And why did Count Brass look so much younger? Why did he seem unaware that he possessed a daughter?

"Not warned by whom?" said Hawkmoon insistently. If it came to a fight he knew that Count Brass could easily defeat him. Count Brass had ever been the best fighter in Europe. Even in late middle-age there had been no one who could begin to match him in a man-to-man sword engagement.

"By the oracle. And another thing puzzles me, my enemy to be; why, if you still live, do you, too, dwell in the netherworld?"

"This is not the netherworld. It is the land of the Kamarg. Do you not recognize it, then—you, who were its Lord Guardian for so many years—who helped defend it against the Dark Empire? I do not think you can be Count Brass."

The figure raised a gauntleted hand to its brow in a gesture of puzzlement. "Think you that? Yet we have never met..."

"Not met? We have fought together in many battles. We have saved each other's lives. I think that you are a man who bears a resemblance to Count Brass, who has been trapped by some sorcery or other and taught to think that he *is* Count Brass—then despatched to kill me. Perhaps some remnants of the old Dark Empire still survive. Perhaps some of Queen Flana's subjects still hate me. Does that idea mean anything to you?"

"No. But I know that I am Count Brass. Do not confuse me further, Duke of Köln."

"How do you know you are Count Brass? Because you resemble him?"

"Because I *am* him!" The man roared. "Dead or alive— *I am Count Brass!*"

"How can you be, when you do not recognise me? When you did not even know you had a daughter? When you confuse this land of the Kamarg for some supernatural netherworld? When you recall nothing of what we went through together in the service of the Runestaff? When you believe that I, of all people, who loved you, whose life and dignity both were saved by you, should have betrayed you?"

"I know nothing of the events of which you speak. But I know of my travellings and of my battles in the service of a score of princes—in Magyaria, Arabia, Scandia, Slavia and the lands of the Greeks and Bulgars. I know of my dream, which is to bring unity to the squabbling princedoms of Europe. I know of my successes—aye, and of my failures, too. I know of the women I have loved, of the friends I have had—and of the enemies I have fought. And I know, too, that you are neither friend nor foe as yet, but will become my most treacherous enemy. On Earth I lie dying. Here I travel in search of the one who will finally take all I possess, including my very life."

"And say again who has granted you this boon?"

"Gods—supernatural beings—the oracle itself—I know not."

"You believe in such things?"

"I did not. Now I must, for the evidence is here."

"I think not. I am not dead. I do not inhabit a netherworld. I am flesh and blood and so, by the looks of it, are you, my friend. I hated you when I first rode out to seek you. Now I see that you are as much a victim as am I. Return to your masters. Tell them that it is Hawkmoon who shall be avenged—upon them!"

"By Narsha's garter, I'll not be given orders!" roared the man in brass. His gloved right hand fell upon the hilt of his sword. It was a gesture typical of Count Brass. The expressions were Count Brass's too. Was this some terrible simulacrum of the Count, invented by Dark Empire science?

Hawkmoon was by now almost hysterical with bewilderment and grief.

"Very well, then," he cried, "let us go to it, you and I.

If you are truly Count Brass you'll have little difficulty in slaying me. Then you will be content. And so will I, for I could not live with people suspecting that I had betrayed you!"

But then the man's expression changed and became thoughtful. "I am Count Brass, be certain of that, Duke of Köln. But, as for the rest, it is possible that we are both victims of a plot. I have not merely been a soldier in my life, but a politician, too. I know of those who delight in turning friend against friend for their own ends. There is a slight possibility that you speak truth..."

"Well, then," said Dorian Hawkmoon in relief, "return with me to Castle Brass and we will discuss what we both know."

The man shook his head. "No, I cannot. I have seen the lights of your walled city and your castle above it. I would visit it—but there is something that stops me from so doing—a barrier. I cannot explain what its properties are. That is why I have been forced to wait for you in this damned marsh. I had hoped to get this business over with swiftly, but now..." The man frowned again. "For all that I am a practical man, Duke of Köln, I have always prided myself on being a just one. I would not slay you to fulfil some other's end—not unless knew what that end was, at any rate. I must consider all that you have said. Then if I decide that you are lying to save your skin, I will kill you."

"Or," said Hawkmoon grimly, "if you are not Count Brass, there is a good chance that I shall kill you."

The man smiled a familiar smile—Count Brass's smile. "Aye—if I am not Count Brass," he said.

"I shall come back to the marsh at noon tomorrow," said Hawkmoon. "Where shall we meet?"

"Noon? There is no noon here. No sun at all!"

"In this you do lie," Hawkmoon laughed. "In a few hours it will be morning here."

Again the man passed a gauntleted hand across his frowning brow. "Not for me," he said. "Not for me."

This puzzled Hawkmoon all the more. "But you have been here for days, I heard."

"A night—a long, perpetual night."

"Does this fact, too, not make you believe you are the victim of a deception?"

"It might," said the man. He gave a deep sigh. "Well, come when you think. Do you see yonder ruin—on the hillock?" He pointed with a finger of brass.

In the moonlight Hawkmoon could just make out the shape of an old ruined building which Bowgentle had described as being that of a Gothic church of immense age. It had been one of Count Brass's favourite places. He had often ridden there when he felt the need to be alone.

"I know the ruin," said Hawkmoon.

"Then meet me there. I shall wait as long as my patience lasts."

"Very well."

"And come armed," said the man, "for we shall probably need to fight."

"You are not convinced of what I have said?"

"You have said nothing very much, friend Hawkmoon. Vague suppositions. References to people I do not know. You think the Dark Empire is bothered with us? It has more important matters to consider, I should think."

"The Dark Empire is destroyed. You helped destroy it."

And again the man grinned a familiar grin. "That is where you are deceived, Duke of Köln." He turned his horse and began to ride back into the night.

"Wait!" called Hawkmoon. "What do you mean?"

But the man had begun to gallop now.

Wildly, Hawkmoon spurred his horse in pursuit. "What do you mean?"

The horse was reluctant to go at such a pace. It snorted

and tried to pull back, but Hawkmoon spurred the beast harder. "Wait!"

He could just see the rider ahead, but his outline was becoming less well-defined. Surely he could not truly be a ghost?

"Wait!"

Hawkmoon's horse slipped in the slime. It whinnied in fear, as if trying to warn Hawkmoon of their mutual danger. Hawkmoon spurred the horse again. It reared. Its hind-legs began to slip in the mud.

Hawkmoon tried to control his steed, but it was falling and taking him with it.

And then they had both plunged off the narrow marsh road, broken through the reeds at the edge and fallen heavily into mud which gulped greedily and tugged them to itself. Hawkmoon tried to struggle back to the bank, but his feet were still in his stirrups and one of his legs was trapped beneath the bulk of his horse's floundering body.

He stretched out and grabbed at a bunch of reeds, trying to drag himself to safety, he moved a few inches towards the path and then the reeds were wrenched free and he fell back.

He became calm as he realised that he was being pulled deeper and deeper into the swamp with every panicky movement.

He reflected that if he did have enemies who wished to see him dead he had, in his own stupidity, granted their wish, after all.

chapter three

A LETTER FROM QUEEN FLANA

He could not see his horse, but he could hear it.

The poor beast was snorting as the mud filled its mouth. Its struggles had grown much weaker.

Hawkmoon had managed to free his feet from the stirrups and his leg was no longer trapped, but now only his arms, his head and his shoulders were above the surface. Little by little he was slipping to his death.

He had had some notion of climbing on to the horse's back and from there leaping to the path, but his efforts in that direction had been entirely unsuccessful. All he had done was push the animal a little further under. Now the horse's breathing was ugly, muffled, painful. Hawkmoon knew that his own breathing would soon sound the same.

He felt completely impotent. By his own foolishness he had got himself into this position. Far from solving anything, he had created a further problem. And, if he died, he knew,

too, that many would say that he had been slain by Count
Brass's ghost. This would give credence to the accusations
of Czernik and the others. It would mean that Yisselda
herself would be suspected of helping him betray her own
father. At best she could leave Castle Brass, perhaps going
to live with Queen Flana, perhaps going to Köln. It would
mean that his son Manfred would not inherit his birthright
as Lord Guardian of the Kamarg. It would mean that his
daughter Yarmila would be ashamed to speak his name.

"I am a fool," he said aloud. "And a murderer. For I
have slain a good horse besides myself. Perhaps Czernik
was right—perhaps the Black Jewel made me do acts of
treachery I cannot now remember. Perhaps I deserve to die."

And then he thought he heard Count Brass ride by, mock-
ing him with ghostly laughter. But it was probably only a
marsh goose whose slumber had been disturbed by a fox.

Now his left arm was being sucked down. Carefully he
raised it. Even the reeds were out of reach now.

He heard his horse give one last sigh as its head sank
beneath the mud. He saw its body heave as it sought to
draw breath. And then it was still. He watched as its torso
slipped from sight.

Now there were more ghostly voices to mock him. Was
that Yisselda's voice? The cry of a gull. And the deeper
voices of his soldiers? The bark of foxes and marsh bears.

This deception seemed, at that moment, to be the cruel-
lest of all—for his own brain deceived him.

Again he was filled with a sense of irony. To have fought
for so long and so hard against the Dark Empire. To have
survived terrifying adventures on two continents—only to
die in ignominy, alone, in a swamp. None would know
where or how he had died. His grave would be unmarked.
There would be no statue erected to him outside the walls
of Castle Brass. Well, he thought, it was a quiet way to
die, at least.

"Dorian!"

This time the bird's cry seemed to call his name. He called back at it, echoing it. "Dorian!"

"Dorian!"

"My Lord of Köln," said the voice of a marsh bear.

"My Lord of Köln," said Hawkmoon in the same tone. Now it was completely impossible to free his left arm. He felt the mud burying his chin. The constricting mud against his chest made it that much harder for him to breath. He felt dizzy. He hoped that he might become unconscious before the mud filled his mouth.

Perhaps if he died he would find that he dwelled in some netherworld. Perhaps he would meet Count Brass again. And Oladahn of the Bulgar Mountains. And Huillam D'Averc. And Bowgentle, the philosopher, the poet.

"Ah," he said to himself, "If I could be sure, then I would welcome this death a little more readily. Yet, there is still the question of my honour—and that of Yisselda. Yisselda!"

"Dorian!" Again the bird's cry bore an uncanny resemblance to his wife's voice. He had heard that dying men entertained such fancies. Perhaps for some it made death easier, but for him it made it that much harder.

"Dorain! I thought I heard you speak. Are you near by? What has happened."

Hawkmoon called back to the bird. "I am in the marsh, my love, and I am dying. Tell them that Hawkmoon was not a traitor. Tell them he was not a coward. Tell them, instead, that he was a fool!"

The reeds near the bank began to rustle. Hawkmoon looked towards them, expecting to see a fox. That would be terrible, to be attacked even as the mud dragged him under. He shuddered.

And then there was a human face peering at him through the reeds. And it was a face he recognised.

"Captain?"

"My Lord," said Captain Josef Vedla. Then his face turned away as he spoke to someone behind him. "You were right, my lady. He is here. And almost completely under." A brand flared as Vedla extended it out as far as he could stretch, peering at Hawkmoon to see just how far he was buried. "Quickly, men—the rope."

"I am pleased to see you, Captain Vedla. Is my lady Yisselda with you, too?"

"I am, Dorian." Her voice was tense. "I found Captain Vedla and he took me to the tavern where Czernik was. It was Czernik who told us that you had ventured into the marsh. So we gathered what men we could and came to find you."

"I am grateful," said Hawkmoon, "though I should not have been if I had not acted so foolishly—ugh!" The mud had reached his mouth.

A rope was flung towards him. With his free right hand he just managed to grasp it and stick his wrist through the loop.

"Pull away," he said, and groaned as the noose tightened on his wrist and he felt as if his arm were being dragged from its socket.

Slowly his body emerged from the mud, which was reluctant to give up its feast, until he was able to sit gasping on the bank while Yisselda, careless that he was covered in the slimy, stinking stuff from head to toe, embraced him, sobbing. "We thought you dead."

"I thought myself dead," he said. "Instead I have killed one of my best horses. I deserve to die."

Captain Vedla was looking nervously about him. Unlike the guardians who were Kamarg bred, he had never been much attracted to the marsh, even in daylight.

"I saw the fellow who calls himself Count Brass." Hawkmoon addressed Captain Vedla.

"And you killed him, my lord?"

Hawkmoon shook his head. "I think he's some play-actor who bears a strong resemblance to Count Brass. But he is not Count Brass—living or dead—of that I'm almost certain. He's too young, for one thing. And he had not been properly educated in his part. He does not know the name of his daughter. He knows nothing of the Kamarg. Yet, I think, there is no malice in the fellow. He might be mad, but more likely he's been mesmerised into believing that he is Count Brass. Some Dark Empire trouble-makers, I'd guess, out to discredit me and avenge themselves at the same time."

Vedla looked relieved. "At least I will have something to tell the gossip-mongers," he said. "But this fellow must have had a startling resemblance to the old Count if he deceived Czernik."

"Aye—he was everything—expressions, gestures and so on. But there is something a little vague about his manner—as if he is in a dream. That is what led me to suspect that he is not, himself, acting maliciously but had been put up to this by others." Hawkmoon got up.

"Where is this impostor now?" Yisselda asked.

"He disappeared into the marsh. I was following him—at too great a speed—when this happened to me." Hawkmoon laughed. "I had become so worried, you know, that I thought for a moment he really had disappeared—like a ghost."

Yisselda smiled. "You can have my horse," she said. "I will ride on your lap, as I have done more than once before."

And in a much relaxed mood the small party returned to Castle Brass.

By the next morning the story of Dorian Hawkmoon's encounter with the "play-actor" had spread throughout the town and among the ambassadorial guests in the castle. It had become a joke. Everyone was relieved to be able to

laugh, to mention it without danger of giving offence to
Hawkmoon. And the festivities went on, growing wilder as
the wind blew stronger. Hawkmoon, now that he had nothing to fear for his honour, decided to make the false Count
Brass wait for a day or two and this he did, throwing himself
completely into the merry-making.

But then, one morning at breakfast, while Hawkmoon
and his guests decided on their plans for that day, young
Lonson of Shkarlan came down with a letter in his hand.
The letter bore many seals and looked most impressive. "I
received this today, my lord," said Lonson. "It came by
ornithopter from Londra. It is from the queen herself."

"News from Londra. Splendid." Hawkmoon accepted the
letter and began to break the seals. "Now, Prince Lonson,
sit and break your fast while I read."

Prince Lonson smiled and, at Yisselda's suggestion, sat
beside the lady of the castle, helping himself to a steak from
the platter before him.

Hawkmoon began to read Queen Flana's letter. There
was general news of the progress of her schemes for farming
large areas of her nation. These seemed to be going well.
Indeed, in some cases they had surpluses which they were
able to trade with Normandia and Hanoveria, whose own
farming was going well, too. But it was towards the end of
the letter that Hawkmoon began to give it more attention.

"And so we come to the only unpleasant detail of this
letter, my dear Dorian. It seems that my efforts to rid
my country of reminders of its dark past have not been
entirely successful. Mask-wearing has sprung up again.
There has been some attempt, I gather, to re-form
some of the old Beast Orders—particularly the Order
of the Wolf of which, you will recall, Baron Meliadus

was Grand Master. Some of my own agents have, upon occasions, been able to disguise themselves as members of the cult and gain entry to meetings. An oath is sworn which might amuse you (I hope, indeed, that it will not disturb you!)—as well as swearing to bring back the Dark Empire in all its glory, to oust me from my throne and to destroy all those loyal to me, they also swear vengeance upon you and your family. Those who survived the Battle of Londra, they say, must all be wiped out. In your secure Kamarg, I doubt if you are in much danger from a few Granbretanian dissidents, so I advise you to continue to sleep well! I know for certaih that these secret cults are not much popular and only flourish in those parts of Londra not yet rebuilt. The great majority of the people—aristocrats and commoners alike—have taken happily to rural life and to parliamentary government. It was our old way to rule thus, when Granbretan was sane. I hope that we are sane again and that, soon, even those few pockets of insanity will be cleansed from our society. One other peculiar rumour, which my agents have been unable to verify, is that some of the worst of the Dark Empire lords are still alive somewhere and waiting to resume their "rightful place as rulers of Granbretan". I cannot believe this—it seems to be a typical legend invented by the disinherited. There must be a thousand heroes sleeping in caves all over Granbretan alone, waiting to spring to somebody's assistance when the time is ripe (why is it never ripe, I wonder!). To be on the safe side, my agents are trying to find the source of these rumours, but several, I regret to say, have already died as the cultists discover their true identities. It should take several months, but I think we shall soon be completely rid of the mask-wearers, particularly since the dark places they prefer to inhabit are being torn down very rapidly indeed."

"Is there disturbing news in Flana's letter?" Yisselda asked her husband as he folded the parchment.

He shook his head. "Not really. It just fits with something that I heard recently. She says that mask-wearing has sprung up again in Londra."

"But that is bound to happen for a while, surely? Is it widespread?"

"Apparently not."

Prince Lonson laughed. "There is surprisingly little of it, my lady, I assure you. Most of the ordinary people were only too pleased to rid themselves of uncomfortable masks and heavy clothes. This is true, too, of the nobility—save for the few who were members of warrior-castes and still survived (happily there were not many)."

"Flana says that there are rumours of some of the prime movers among them still being alive," said Hawkmoon quietly.

"Impossible. You slew Baron Meliadus himself—*split*, Duke of Köln, from shoulder to groin!"

One or two of the other guests looked rather put out by Prince Lonson's remark. He apologised profusely. "Count Brass," he continued, "despatched Adaz Promp and several more. Shenegar Trott you also slew, in Dnark, before the Runestaff. And the others—Mikosevaar, Nankenseen and the rest—all are dead. Taragorm died in an explosion and Kalan killed himself. What others are left?"

Hawkmoon frowned. "All I can think of are Taragorm and Kalan," he said. "They are the only two whose deaths were unwitnessed."

"But Taragorm died in an explosion of Kalan's battle-machine. None could have survived it."

"You are right." Hawkmoon smiled. "It is silly to speculate like this. There are better things to do."

And again he turned his attention to the day's festivities.

But that night, he knew, he would ride out to the ruin and confront the one who called himself Count Brass.

chapter four

A COMPANY OF THE DEAD

Thus it was at sunset that Dorian Hawkmoon, Duke of Köln, Lord Guardian of the Kamarg, rode out again upon the winding marsh roads, deep into his domain, watching the scarlet flamingoes wheel, seeing the herds of white bulls and horned horses in the distance, like clouds of fast-flowing smoke passing through the green and tawny reeds, seeing the lagoons turned to pools of blood by the red and sinking sun. Breathing the sharp air borne by the mistral, and coming at last to a small hill on which stood a ruin of immense age—a ruin around which ivy, purple and amber, climbed. And there, as the last rays of the sun died, Dorian Hawkmoon dismounted from his horned horse and waited for a ghost to come.

The wind tugged at his high-collared cloak. It blew at his face and froze his lips. It made the hairs of his horse's coat ripple like water. It keened across the wide, flat marshlands. And, as the day animals began to compose themselves for slumber, and before the night animals began to merge, there fell upon the great Kamarg a terrible stillness.

Even the wind dropped. The reeds no longer rustled. Nothing moved.

And Hawkmoon waited on.

Much later he heard the sound of a horse's hooves on the damp marshland ground. A muffled sound. He reached over to his left hip and loosened his broadsword in its scabbard. He was in armour now. Steel armour which had been made to fit every contour of his body. He brushed hair from his eyes and adjusted his plain helm—as plain as Count Brass's own. He threw back the cloak from his shoulders so that it should not encumber his movements.

But there was more than one horseman approaching. He listened carefully. The moon was full tonight but the riders came from the other side of the ruin and he could see nothing of them. He counted. Four horsemen, by the sound of it. So—the impostor had brought allies. It had been a trap, after all. Hawkmoon sought cover. The only cover was in the ruin itself. Cautiously he moved towards it, clambering over the old, worn stones until he was certain that he was hidden from anyone who came from either side of the hill. Only the horse betrayed his presence.

The riders came up the hill. He could see them now, in silhouette. They rode their horses straight-backed. There was a pride in their stance. Who could they be?

Hawkmoon saw a glint of brass and knew that one of them was the false Count. But the other three wore no distinctive armour. They reached the top of the hill and saw his horse.

He heard the voice of Count Brass calling:

"Duke von Köln?"

Hawkmoon did not reply.

He heard another voice. A languid voice. "Perhaps he has gone to relieve himself in yonder ruin?"

And, with a shock, Hawkmoon recognised that voice too.

It was the voice of Huillam D'Averc. Dead D'Averc, who had died so ironically in Londra.

He saw the figure approach, a handkerchief in one hand, and he recognised the face, too. It was D'Averc's. Then Hawkmoon knew, terrifyingly, who the other two riders were.

"Wait for him. He said he'd come, did he not, Count Brass?" Bowgentle was speaking now.

"Aye. He said so."

"Then I hope he hurries, for this wind bites even through *my* thick pelt." Oladahn's voice.

And Hawkmoon knew then that this was a nightmare, whether he slept or whether he was awake. It was the most painful experience of his life to see those who so closely resembled his dead friends walking and talking as they had walked and talked in each other's company some five years since. Hawkmoon would have given his own life if it would have brought them back, but he knew that it was impossible. No kind of resurrection drug could revive one who, like Oladahn of the Bulgar Mountains, had been torn to pieces and those pieces scattered. And there were no signs of wounds on the others, either.

"I shall catch a chill, that's certain—and die a second time, perhaps." This was D'Averc, typically thoughtful for his own health, which was as robust as anyone's. Were these ghosts?

"What has brought us together, I wonder," mused Bowgentle. "And to such a bleak and sunless world? We met once, I believe, Count Brass—at Rouen, was it not? At the Court of Hanal the White?"

"I believe so."

"By the sound of him, this Duke of Köln is worse than Hanal for indiscriminate bloodletting. The only thing we have in common, as far as I can tell, is that we shall all die by his hand if we do not kill him now. Yet, it is hard to believe..."

"He suggested that we were the victims of a plot, as I told you," said Count Brass. "It could be true."

"We are victims of something, that's certain," said D'Averc, blowing his nose delicately upon his lacey handkerchief. "But I agree that it would be best to discuss the matter with our murderer before we despatch him. What if we kill him and nothing comes of it—we remain in this dreadful, gloomy place for eternity—with him as a companion, for he'll be dead, too."

"How did you come to die?" Oladahn asked almost conversationally.

"A sordid death—a mixture of greed and jealousy was my undoing. The greed was mine. The jealousy another's."

"You intrigue us all," laughed Bowgentle.

"A mistress of mine was, it happened, married to another gentleman. She was a splendid cook—her range of recipes was incredible, my friends, both at the stove and in the bed, if you follow me. Well, I was staying with her for a week while her husband was away at Court—this was in Hanoveria where I myself had business at the time. The week was splendid, but it came to an end, for her husband was due to return that night. To console me, my mistress cooked a splendid supper. A triumph! She never cooked a better. There were snails and soups and goulashes and little birds in exquisite sauces and soufflés—well, I see I discomfort you and I apologise.... The meal, in short, was superb. I had more than is good for one of my delicate health and then I begged my mistress while there was still time to favour me with her company in bed for just one short hour, since her husband was not due back for two. With some reluctance she agreed. We fell into bed. We rounded off the meal in ecstasy. We fell asleep. So fast asleep, I might add, that we were only awakened by her husband shaking us awake!"

"And he killed you, eh?" said Oladahn.

"In a manner of speaking. I leapt up. I had no sword. I had no cause to kill him, either, of course, since he was the injured party (and I've a strong sense of justice). Up I jumped and out of the window I dashed. No clothes. Lots of rain. Five miles back to my own lodgings. Result, of course, pneumonia."

Oladahn laughed and the sound of his merriment was agonising to Hawkmoon. "Of which you died?"

"Of which, to be accurate, if that peculiar oracle is correct, I am dying, while my spirit sits on a windy hill and is no better off, it seems!" D'Averc went to shelter beside the ruin and was not five feet from where Hawkmoon crouched. "How did you come to die, my friend?"

"I fell off a rock."

"A high one?"

"No—about ten feet."

"And it killed you?"

"No, it was the bear that killed me. It was waiting below."

Again Oladahn laughed.

And again Hawkmoon felt a pang of pain.

"I died of the Scandian plague," said Bowgentle. "Or am to die of it."

"And I in battle against King Orson's elephants in Tarkia," put in the one who believed himself to be Count Brass.

And Hawkmoon was reminded most strongly of actors preparing themselves for their parts. He would have believed they were actors, too, had it not been for their speech inflections, their gestures, their ways of expressing themselves. There were slight differences, but none to make Hawkmoon suspect these were not his friends. Yet, just as

Count Brass had not known him, so these did not know each other.

Some idea of the possible truth was beginning to dawn on Hawkmoon as he emerged from hiding and confronted them.

"Good evening, gentlemen." He bowed. "I am Dorian Hawkmoon von Köln. I know you Oladahn—and you Bowgentle—and you D'Averc—and we've met already Count Brass. Are you here to slay me?"

"To discuss if we should," said Count Brass, seating himself upon a flat rock. "Now I regard myself as a reasonable judge of men. In fact I'm an exceptionally good judge, or I should not have survived this long. And I do not believe, Dorian Hawkmoon, that you have much treachery in you. Even in a situation which might justify such treachery—or which you would consider as justifying treachery—I doubt if you would be a traitor. And that is what disturbs me about this situation. Secondly, all four of us are known to you but we do not know you. Thirdly we appear to be the only four sent to this particular netherworld and that is a coincidence I mistrust. Fourthly we were each told a similar story—that you would betray us at some future date. Now, assuming that this, itself, is a future date where all five of us have met and become friends, what does that suggest to you?"

"That you are all from my past!" said Hawkmoon. "That is why you look younger to me, Count Brass—and you, Bowgentle—and you, Oladahn—and you, too, D'Averc..."

"Thank you," said D'Averc sardonically.

"Which means that none of us died in the way we think we died—in battle at Tarkia, in my case—of sickness in the castle of Bowgentle and D'Averc—attacked by a bear in the case of Oladahn, here..."

"Exactly," said Hawkmoon, "for I met you all later and you were all very much alive. But I remember you telling me, Oladahn, how once you were nearly killed by a bear—and you told me how close you came to death in Tarkia, Count Brass—and, Bowgentle, I remember some mention of the Scandian plague."

"And I?" asked D'Averc with interest.

"I forget, D'Averc—for your illnesses tended to run into each other and I never saw you anything but in the best of health . . ."

"Ah! Am I to be cured, then?"

Hawkmoon ignored D'Averc and continued. "So this means you are not going to die—though you, yourselves, think that you might. Whoever is deceiving us wants you to think that it is by their efforts that you'll survive."

"Much what I worked out." Count Brass nodded.

"But that's as far as my logic leads me," said Hawkmoon, "for a paradox is involved here—why, when we *did* (or do) meet, did we not remember this particular meeting?"

"We must find our villains and ask them that question, I think," said Bowgentle. "Of course, I have studied something of the nature of time. Such paradoxes, according to one school of thought, would necessarily resolve themselves—memories would be wiped clean of anything which contradicted the normal experience of time. The brain, in short, would sponge out anything which was apparently inconsistent. However, there are certain aspects of that line of reasoning with which I am not wholly happy . . ."

"Perhaps we could discuss the philosophical implications at some other time, Sir Bowgentle," said Count Brass gruffly.

"Time and philosophy are but one subject, Count Brass. And only philosophy may easily discuss the nature of time."

"Perhaps. But there is the other matter—the possibility that we are being manipulated by malicious men who are somehow able to control time. How do we reach them and what do we do when we do reach them?"

"I remember something concerning crystals," mused Hawkmoon, "which transported men through alternate dimensions of the Earth. I wonder if these crystals, or something like them, are being used again?"

"I know nothing of crystals," said Count Brass, and the other three agreed that they knew nothing, either.

"There are other dimensions, you see," Hawkmoon went on. "And it could be that there are dimensions where live men almost identical to men living in this dimension. We found a Kamarg that was not dissimilar to this. I wonder if that is the answer. Yet, still not quite the answer."

"I barely follow you," growled Count Brass. "You begin to sound like this sorcerer fellow . . ."

"Philosopher," corrected Bowgentle, "and poet."

"Aye, it's complicated thinking that's involved if we're to get closer to the truth," said Hawkmoon. He told them the story of Elvereza Tozer and the Crystal Rings of Mygan—how they had been used to transport himself and D'Averc through the dimensions, across seas—perhaps through time itself. And since they all had played parts in this drama, Hawkmoon felt the strangeness of the situation—for he spoke familiarly of them as his friends—and he referred to events which were to take place in their future. And when he was finished they seemed convinced that he had produced a likely explanation for their present situation. Hawkmoon remembered, too, the Wraith-folk, those gentle people who had given him a machine which had helped lift Castle Brass from its own space-time into another, safer space-time when Baron Meliadus attacked them. Perhaps if he were to travel to Soryandum in the Syranian Desert he might again enlist the help of the Wraith-folk. He put this to his friends.

"Aye, an idea worth trying," said Count Brass. "But in

the meantime we're still in the grip of whomever put us here in the first place—and we've no explanation of how they've accomplished that or, for that matter, exactly why they have done it."

"This oracle you spoke of," said Hawkmoon. "Where is it? Can you tell me exactly what happened to you—after you 'died'?"

"I found myself in this land, with all my wounds healed and my armour repaired..."

The others agreed that this was what happened to them.

"With a horse and with food to last me for a good while—though unpalatable stuff it is."

"And the oracle?"

"A sort of speaking pyramid about the height of a man—glowing—diamond-like—hovering above the ground. It appears and vanishes at will, it seems. It told me all that I told you when we first met. I assumed it to be supernatural in origin—though it went against all my previous beliefs..."

"It is probably of mortal origin," said Hawkmoon. "Either the word of some sorcerer-scientist such as those who once worked for the Dark Empire—or else something which our ancestors invented before the Tragic Millennium."

"I've heard of such," agreed Count Brass. "And I prefer that explanation. It suits my temperament more, I must admit."

"Did it offer to restore you to life once I was slain?" Hawkmoon asked.

"Aye—that's it, in short."

"That's what it told me," said D'Averc, and the others nodded.

"Well, perhaps we should confront this machine, if machine it be, and see what happens?" Bowgentle suggested.

"There is another mystery, however," Hawkmoon said.

"Why is it that you are in perpetual night in the Kamarg, whereas, for me, the days pass normally?"

"A splendid conundrum," said D'Averc in some delight. "Perhaps we should ask it. After all, if this is Dark Empire work, they would hardly seek to harm me—I am a friend of Granbretan!"

And Hawkmoon smiled a private smile.

"You are at present, Huillam D'Averc."

"Let's make a plan," said Count Brass practically. "Shall we set off now to see if we can find the diamond pyramid?"

"Wait for me here," said Hawkmoon. "I must return home first. I will be back before dawn—this is, in a few hours. Will you trust me?"

"I'd rather trust a man than a crystal pyramid," smiled Count Brass.

Hawkmoon walked to where his horse grazed. He lifted himself into his saddle.

As he rode away from the little hill, leaving the four men behind him, he forced himself to think as clearly as was possible, trying to avoid considering the paradoxical implications of what he had learned this night and to concentrate on what was likely to have created the situation. There were two possibilities, in his experience, as to what was at work here—the Runestaff on the one hand and the Dark Empire on the other. But it could be neither—some other force. Yet the only other people with great scientific resources were the Wraith-folk of Soryandum and it seemed unlikely that they would concern themselves with the affairs of others. Besides, only the Dark Empire would want him destroyed—by one or all of his now-dead friends. It was an irony which would have suited their perverse minds. Yet—the fact came back to him—all the great leaders of the old Dark Empire were dead. But then so were Count Brass, Oladahn, Bowgentle and D'Averc dead.

Hawkmoon drew a deep breath of cold air into his lungs as the town of Aigues-Mortes came in sight. The thought had already come to him that perhaps even this was a complicated trap and that soon he, too, might be dead.

And that was why he rode back to Castle Brass, to take his leave of his wife, to kiss his children and to write a letter which should be opened if he did not return.

book two

OLD ENEMIES

chapter one

A SPEAKING PYRAMID

Hawkmoon's heart was heavy as he rode away from Castle Brass for the third time. The pleasure he felt at seeing his old friends again was mixed with the painful knowledge that, in one sense, they *were* ghosts. He had seen them dead, all of them. Also these men were strangers. Whereas he recalled conversations, adventures and events they had shared, they knew nothing of these things; they did not know each other, even. Hanging over everything was the knowledge that they would die, in their own futures, and that his being reunited with them might last only a few more hours, whereupon they might be snatched away again by whomever or whatever was manipulating them. It was even possible that when he returned to the ruin on the hill they would already be gone.

That was why he had told Yisselda as little of the night's occurrences as possible, merely letting her know that he must go away, to seek the source of whatever it was that threatened him. The rest he had put in the letter so that, if he did not return, she would learn all of the truth that he knew at this stage. He had not mentioned Bowgentle, D'Averc and Oladahn and had made it plain to her that he considered Count Brass an impostor. He did not want her to share the burden which now lay upon his shoulders.

There were still several hours to go before dawn when he at last reached the hill and saw that four men and four horses waited for him there. He reached the ruin and dismounted. The four came towards him out of the shadows and for an instant he believed that he was really in a netherworld, in the company of the dead, but he dismissed this morbid thought and said, instead:

"Count Brass, something puzzles me."

The Count all clad in brass inclined his brazen head. "And what is that?"

"When we parted—at our first meeting—I told you that the Dark Empire was destroyed. You told me that it was not. This puzzled me so much that I attempted to follow you but, instead, stumbled into the marsh. What did you mean? Do you know more than you have told me?"

"I spoke only the simple truth. The Dark Empire grows in strength. It extends its boundaries."

And then something became clear to Hawkmoon and he laughed. "In what year was the battle of which you spoke—in Tarkia?"

"Why, this year. The sixty-seventh Year of the Bull."

"No, you are wrong," said Bowgentle. "This is the eighty-first Year of the Rat . . ."

"The ninetieth Year of the Frog," said D'Averc.

"The seventy-fifth Year of the Goat," Oladahn contradicted.

"You are all wrong," said Hawkmoon. "This year—the year in which we are now as we stand upon this hillock—is the eighty-ninth Year of the Rat. Therefore, to you all the Dark Empire still thrives, has not even begun to show her full strength. But to me, the Empire is over—pulled down primarily by we four. Now do you see why I suspect that we are the objects of Dark Empire vengeance? Either some Dark Empire sorcerer has looked into the future and seen what we did, or else some sorcerer has escaped the doom we brought to the Beast Lords and is now trying to repay us for the injury we did to them. The five of us came together some six years ago, to serve the Runestaff, of which you have all doubtless heard, against the Dark Empire. We were successful in our mission, but four died to achieve that success—you four. Save for the Wraith-folk of Soryandum, who take no interest in human affairs, the only ones capable of manipulating Time are the Dark Empire sorcerers."

"I have often thought that I should like to know how I was to die," said Count Brass, "but now I am not so sure."

"We have only your word, friend Hawkmoon," said D'Averc. "There are still many mysteries unsolved—among them the fact that if all this is taking place in our future, why did we not recall having met you before when we *did* meet?" He raised his eyebrows and then began to cough into his handkerchief.

Bowgentle smiled. "I have already explained the theory concerning this seeming paradox. Time does not necessarily flow in a linear motion. It is our minds which perceive it flowing in this way. *Pure* Time might even have a random nature . . ."

"Yes, yes," said Oladahn. "Somehow, good Sir Bowgentle, you have a way of confusing me further with your explanations."

"Then let us just say that Time might not be what we think it to be," said Count Brass. "And we've some proof of that, after all, for we do not need to believe Duke Dorian—we have certain knowledge that we were all wrenched from different years and stand together now. Whether we're in the future or the past, it's clear we are in different time-periods to those we left behind. And, of course, this does help to support Duke Dorian's suggestions and to contradict what the pyramid told us."

"I support that logic, Count Brass," Bowgentle agreed. "Both intellectually and emotionally I am inclined to throw in my lot, for the moment, with Duke Dorian. I am not sure what I would have done, anyway, had I planned to kill him, for it goes against all my beliefs to take the life of another being."

"Well, if you two are convinced," said D'Averc yawning. "I am prepared to be. I never was a judge of character. I rarely knew where my real interests lay. As an architect my work, grandly ambitious and minutely paid, was always done for some princeling who was promptly dethroned. His successor never seemed to favour my work—and I had usually insulted the fellow, anyway. As a painter I chose patrons who were inclined to die before they could begin seriously to support me. That is why I became a freelance diplomat—to learn more of the ways of politics before I returned to my old professions. As yet I do not feel I have learned anything like enough . . ."

"Perhaps that is because you prefer to listen to your own voice," said Oladahn gently. "Had not we better set off to seek the pyramid, gentlemen?" He hefted his quiver of arrows on his back and unstrung his bow to loop it over his shoulder. "After all, we do not know how much time we have left."

"You are right. When dawn comes I might see you all vanish." Hawkmoon said. "I should like to know how the days pass normally for me, in their proper cycle, while for you it is eternal night." He returned to his horse and climbed into the saddle. He had saddle-panniers now, full of food. And there were two lances in a scabbard slung at the back of his saddle. The tall horned stallion he rode was the best horse in the stables of Castle Brass. It was called Brand because its eyes flashed like fire.

The others went to their own horses and mounted. Count Brass pointed down the hillock to the south. "There's a hellish sea yonder—uncrossable I was told. It is to its shore we must go and on that shore we shall see the oracle."

"The sea is only the sea into which flows the Rhône," said Hawkmoon mildly. "Called by some the Middle Sea."

Count Brass laughed. "A sea I have crossed a hundred times. I hope you are right, friend Hawkmoon—and I suspect that you are. Oh, I look forward to matching swords with the ones who deceive us!"

"Let us hope that they give us the opportunity," drily said D'Averc. "For I've a feeling—and, of course, I'm not the judge of men that you are, Count Brass—that we shall have little opportunity for swordplay when dealing with our foes. Their weapons are likely to be a little more sophisticated."

Hawkmoon indicated the tall lances protruding from the rear of his saddle. "I have two flame-lances here, for I anticipated the same situation."

"Well, flame-lances are better than nothing," agreed D'Averc, but he still looked sceptical.

"I have never much favoured sorcerous weapons," said Oladahn with a suspicious glance at the lances. "They are inclined to bring stronger forces against those who wield them."

"You are superstitious, Oladahn. Flame-lances are not the products of supernatural sorcery, but of the science which flourished before the coming of the Tragic Millennium." Bowgentle spoke kindly.

"Aye," said Oladahn. "I think that proves my point, Master Bowgentle."

Soon the dark sea could be seen glinting ahead.

Hawkmoon felt his stomach muscles tighten as he anticipated the encounter with the mysterious pyramid which had tried to get his friends to kill him.

But the shore, when they reached it, was empty save for a few clumps of seaweed, some tufts of grass growing on sandhills, the surf which lapped the beach. Count Brass took them to where he had erected an awning of his cloak behind a sandhill. Here was his food and some of the equipment he had left behind when he set out to meet Hawkmoon. On the way the four had told Hawkmoon how they had come to meet, each, at first, mistaking another for Hawkmoon and challenging him.

"This is where it appears, when it appears," Count Brass said. "I suggest you hide in yonder patch of reeds, Duke Dorian. Then I'll tell the pyramid that we have killed you and we'll see what happens."

"Very well." Hawkmoon unshipped the flame-lances and led his horse into the cover of the tall reeds. From a distance he saw the four men talking for a while and then he heard Count Brass's great voice calling out:

"Oracle! Where are you? You may release me now. The deed is done! Hawkmoon is dead."

Hawkmoon wondered if the pyramid, or those who manipulated it, had any means of testing the truth of Count Brass's words. Did they peer into the whole of this world or merely a part of it. Did they have human spies working for them?

"Oracle!" called Count Brass again. "Hawkmoon is dead by my hand!"

It seemed to Hawkmoon then that they had entirely failed to deceive the so-called oracle. The mistral continued to howl across the lagoons and the marshes. The sea whipped at the shore. Grass and reeds waved. Dawn was fast approaching. Soon the first grey light would begin to appear and then his friends might vanish altogether.

"Oracle! Where are you?"

Something flickered, but it was probably only a wind-borne firefly. Then it flickered again, in the same place, in the air just above Count Brass's head.

Hawkmoon slipped a flame-lance into his hand and felt for the stud which, when pressed, would discharge ruby fire.

"Oracle!"

An outline appeared, white and tenuous. This was the source of the flickering light. It was the outline of a pyramid. And within the pyramid was a fainter shadow which was gradually obscured as the outline began to fill in.

And then a diamond-like pyramid about the height of a man was hovering above Count Brass's head and to his right.

Hawkmoon strained both ears and eyes as the pyramid began to speak.

"You have done well, Count Brass. For this we will send you and your companions back to the world of the living. Where is Hawkmoon's corpse."

Hawkmoon was astonished. He had recognised the voice from the pyramid but he could hardly believe it.

"Corpse?" Count Brass was non-plussed. "You did not speak of his corpse? Why should you? You work in my interest, not I in yours. That is what you told me."

"But the corpse..." The voice was almost pettish now.

"Here is the corpse, Kalan of Vitall!" And Hawkmoon rose from the reeds and strode towards the pyramid. "Show yourself to me, coward. So you did not kill yourself, after all. Well, let me help you now..." And, in his anger, he pressed the stud of the flame-lance and the red fire leapt out from the ruby tip and splashed against the pulsing pyramid so that it howled and then it whined and then it whimpered and became transparent so that the cringing creature within could be seen by all of the five who watched.

"Kalan!" Hawkmoon recognised the Dark Empire scientist. "I guessed it must be you. None saw you die. All thought that the pool of matter left on the floor of your laboratory must be your remains. But you deceived us!"

"It is too hot!" screamed Kalan. "This machine is a delicate thing. You'll destroy it."

"Should I care?"

"Aye—the consequences . . . They would be terrible."

But Hawkmoon continued to play the ruby fire over the pyramid and Kalan continued to cringe and to scream.

"How did you make these poor fellows think it was a netherworld they inhabited. How did you make it perpetual night for them?"

Kalan wailed: "How do you think? I merely made a split-second of their days so that they did not even notice the sun's passing. I speeded up their days and I slowed down their nights."

"And how did you make the barrier which meant they could not reach Castle Brass or the town?"

"Just as easy. Ah! Ah! Every time they reached the walls of the city, I shifted them back a few minutes so that they might never quite reach the walls. These were crude skills— but I warn you, Hawkmoon, the machine is not crude—it is hyperdelicate. It could go out of control and destroy us all."

"As long as I could be sure of your destruction, Kalan, I would not care!"

"You are cruel, Hawkmoon!"

And Hawkmoon laughed at the note of accusation in Kalan's voice. Kalan—who had implanted the Black Jewel in his skull—who had helped Taragorm destroy the crystal machine which had protected Castle Brass—who had been the greatest and most evil of the genuises who had supplied the Dark Empire with its scientific power—accusing Hawkmoon of cruelty.

And the ruby fire continued to play over the pyramid.

"You are wrecking my controls!" Kalan screamed. "If I leave now I shan't be able to return until I have made repairs. I will not be able to release these friends of yours..."

"I think we can do without your help, little man!" Count Brass laughed. "Though I thank you for your concern. You sought to deceive us and now you are paying the price."

"I spoke the truth—Hawkmoon will lead you to your deaths."

"Aye—but they'll be noble deaths and not the fault of Hawkmoon."

Kalan's face twisted. He was sweating as the pyramid grew hotter and hotter. "Very well. I retreat. But I'll take my vengeance on all four of you yet—alive or dead, I'll still reach you all. Now I return..."

"To Londra?" Hawkmoon cried. "Are you hidden in Londra?"

Kalan laughed wildly. "Londra? Aye—but no Londra that you know. Farewell, horrid Hawkmoon."

And the pyramid faded and then vanished and left the five standing on the shore in silence, for there seemed nothing to say at that stage.

A little while later Hawkmoon pointed to the horizon.

"Look," he said.

The sun was beginning to rise.

chapter two

THE RETURN OF THE PYRAMID

For a while, as they breakfasted on the unpalatable food Kalan of Vitall had left for Count Brass and the others, they debated what they must do.

It had become obvious that the four were stranded, for the present, in Hawkmoon's time-period. How long they could remain there none knew.

"I spoke of Soryandum and the Wraith-folk," Hawkmoon told his friends. "It is our only hope of getting help, for the Runestaff is unlikely to give us aid, even if we could find it to ask for such aid." He had told them much of the events which were to occur in their futures and had taken place in his past.

"Then we should make haste," said Count Brass, "lest Kalan returns—as return, I'm sure, he will. How shall we reach Soryandum?"

"I do not know," Hawkmoon said honestly. "They shifted

their city out of our dimensions when the Dark Empire threatened them. I can only hope that they have moved it back to its old location now that the threat had passed."

"And where is Soryandum—or where was it?" Oladahn asked.

"In the Syranian Desert."

Count Brass raised his red eyebrows. "A wide desert, friend Hawkmoon. A vast desert. And harsh."

"Aye. All of those things. That is why so few travellers ever came upon Soryandum."

"And you expect us to cross such a desert in search of a city which *might* be there? D'Averc smiled sourly.

"Aye. It is our only hope, Sir Huillam."

D'Averc shrugged and turned away. "Perhaps the dry air would be good for my chest."

"So we must cross the Middle Sea, then?" said Bowgentle. "We need a boat."

"There is a port not far from here," said Hawkmoon. "There we should find a boat to take us on the long journey to the coasts of Syrania—to the port of Hornus, if possible. After that we journey inland, on camels if we can hire them, beyond the Euphrates."

"A journey of many weeks," said Bowgentle thoughtfully. "Is there no quicker route?"

"This is the quickest. Ornithopters would fly faster, but they are notoriously capricious and have not the range we need. The riding flamingoes of the Kamarg would have offered us an alternative but, I fear, I do not want to draw attention to us in the Kamarg—it would cause too much confusion and pain to those we all love—or will love. Therefore we must go in disguise to Marshais, the largest port hereabouts, and take passage as ordinary travelers aboard the first available ship."

"I see that you have considered this carefully." Count Brass rose and began to pack his gear into his saddlebags.

"We'll follow your plan, my lord of Köln, and hope that we are not traced by Kalan before we reach Soryandum."

Two days later they came, cloaked and cautious, into the bustling city of Marshais, perhaps the greatest seaport on this coast. In the harbour were over a hundred ships—far-going, tall-masted trading vessels, used to plying all kinds of seas in all kinds of weather. And the men, too, were fit to sail in such ships—bronzed by wind, sun and sea, tough, hard-eyed, harsh-voiced seamen for the most part, who kept their own counsel. Many were stripped to the waist, wearing only divided kilts of silk or cotton, dyed in dozens of different shades, with anklets and wristlets often of precious metal studded with gem-stones. And around their necks and heads were tied long scarves, as brightly coloured as their britches. Many wore weapons at their belts—knives and cutlasses for the most part. And most of these men were worth only what they wore—but what they wore, in the way of bracelets and earrings and the like, was worth a small fortune and might be gambled away in a few hours ashore in any of the scores of taverns, inns, gaming houses and whorehouses which lined all the streets leading down to the quays of Marshais.

Into all this noise and bustle and colour came the five weary men, their hoods about their faces, for they wanted none to recognise them. And Hawkmoon knew, best of all, that they would be recognised—five heroes whose portraits hung on many an inn-sign, whose statues filled many a square, whose names were used for the swearing of oaths and for the telling of yarns which could never be as incredible as the truth. There was only one danger that Hawkmoon could see—that in their unwillingness to show their faces they might be mistaken for Dark Empire men, unrepentant and still desiring to hide their heads in masks. They found an inn, quieter than most, in the backstreets and asked for a large room in which they might all stay for a night while one of them went down to the quayside to enquire about a ship.

It was Hawkmoon, who had been growing a beard as they travelled, who elected to make the necessary enquiries and soon after they had eaten he left for the waterfront and returned quite quickly with good news. There was a trader leaving by the first tide of the morning. He was willing to take passengers and charged a reasonable fee. He was not going to Hornus but to Behruk a little further up the coast. This was almost as good and Hawkmoon had decided on the spot to book passages for them all aboard his ship. They all lay down to sleep as soon as this was settled, but none slept well, for there was ever the thought to plague them that the pyramid with Kalan in it would return.

Hawkmoon realised of what the pyramid had reminded him. It was something like the Throne-Globe of the King-Emperor Huon—the thing which had supported the life of that incredibly ancient humanculus before he had been slain by Baron Meliadus. Perhaps the same science had created both? It was more than likely. Or had Kalan found a cache of old machines, such as were buried in many places upon the planet, and used them? And where was Kalan of Vitall hiding? Not in Londra but in some other Londra? Is that what he meant?

Hawkmoon slept poorest of all that night as these thoughts and a thousand others sped through his head. And his sword lay, unscabbarded, in his hand when he did sleep.

On a clear autumn day they set sail in a tall, fast ship called *The Romanian Queen* (Her home port was on the Black Sea) whose sails and decks gleamed white and clean and who seemed to speed without effort over the water.

The sailing was good for the first two days, but on the third day the wind dropped and they were becalmed. The captain was reluctant to unship his vessel's oars, for he had a small crew and did not want to overwork them, so he decided to risk a day's wait and hope that the wind would come up. The coast of Kyprus, an island kingdom which, like so many, had once been a vassal state of the Dark Empire, could just be seen off to the east and it was frustrating for the five friends to have to peer through the narrow porthole of their cabin and see it. All five had remained below decks for the whole voyage. Hawkmoon had explained this strange behaviour by saying that they were members of a religious cult making a pilgrimage and according to their vows, must spend their whole waking time in prayer. The captain, a decent sailor who wanted only a fair price for the passage and no trouble from his passengers, accepted this explanation without question.

It was about noon on the next day, when a wind had still not materialised, that Hawkmoon and the others heard a commotion above their heads—shouts and oaths and running of booted and bare feet to and fro.

"What can it be?" Hawkmoon said. "Pirates? We have met with pirates before in near-by waters, have we not Oladahn?"

But Oladahn merely looked astonished. "Eh? This is my first sea voyage, Duke Dorian!"

And Hawkmoon, not for the first time, remembered that Oladahn was still to experience the adventure of the Mad God's ship, and he apologised to the little mountain man.

The commotion grew louder and more confused. Staring through the porthole, they could see no sign of an attacking ship and there were no sounds of battle. Perhaps some seamonster, some creature left over from the Tragic Millennium, had risen from the waters outside their field of vision?

Hawkmoon rose and put on his cloak, drawing the cowl over his head. "I'll investigate," he said.

He opened the door of the cabin and climbed the short stairway to the deck. And there, near the stern, was the object of the crew's terror, and from it came the voice of Kalan of Vitall exhorting the men to fall upon their passengers and slay them immediately or the whole ship would go down.

The pyramid was glowing a brilliant, blinding white and stood out sharply against the blue of the sky and the sea.

At once Hawkmoon dashed back into the cabin and picked up a flame-lance.

"The pyramid has come back!" he told them. "Wait here while I deal with it."

He climbed the companionway and rushed across the deck towards the pyramid, his passage encumbered by the frightened crewmen who were backing away rapidly.

Again a beam of red light darted from the ruby tip of the flame-lance and splashed against the white of the pyramid, like blood mingling with milk. But this time there were no screams from within the pyramid, only laughter.

"I have taken precautions, Dorian Hawkmoon, against your crude weapons. I have strengthened my machine."

"Let us see to what degree," Hawkmoon said grimly. He had guessed that Kalan was nervous of using his machine's power to manipulate time, that perhaps Kalan was unsure of the results he would achieve.

And now Oladahn of the Bulgar Mountains was beside him, a sword in his furry hand, a scowl on his face.

"Begone, false oracle!" shouted Oladahn. "We do not fear you now."

"You should have cause to fear me," said Kalan, his face now just visible through the semi-transparent material of the pyramid. He was sweating. Plainly the flame-lance was having at least some effect. "For I have the means of controlling all events in this world—and in others!"

"Then control them!" Hawkmoon challenged, and he

turned the beam of his flame-lance to full strength.

"Aaah! Fools—destroy my machine and you disrupt the fabric of time itself. All will be thrown into flux—chaos will rage throughout the universe. All intelligence shall die!"

And then Oladahn was running at the pyramid, his sword whirling, trying to cut through the peculiar substance which protected Kalan from the powers of the flame-lance.

"Get back, Oladahn!" Hawkmoon cried. "You can do nothing with a sword!"

But Oladahn hacked twice at the pyramid and he stabbed through it, it seemed, and almost ran Kalan of Vitall through before the sorcerer turned and saw him and adjusted a small pyramid he held in his hand, grinning at Oladahn with horrible malice.

"Oladahn! Beware!" Hawkmoon yelled, sensing some new danger.

Again Oladahn drew back his arm for another blow at Kalan.

Oladahn screamed.

He looked about him in bewilderment as if he saw something other than the pyramid and the deck of the ship. "The bear!" he wailed. "It has me!"

And then, with a chilling shout, he vanished.

Hawkmoon dropped the flame-lance and ran forward, but he had only a glimpse of Kalan's chuckling features before the pyramid, too, had disappeared.

There was nothing of Oladahn to be seen. And Hawkmoon knew that, initially at least, the little man had been thrown back to the moment he had first left his own time. But would he be allowed to remain there?

Hawkmoon would not have cared so much—for he knew that Oladahn had survived the fight with the bear—if he had not become suddenly aware of the great power which Kalan wielded.

In spite of himself, Hawkmoon shuddered. He turned and saw that both captain and crew were offering him strange suspicious looks.

Without speaking to them he went straight back to his cabin.

Now it had become more urgent than ever that they should find Soryandum and the Wraith-folk.

chapter three

THE JOURNEY TO SORYANDUM

Soon after the incident on deck the wind sprang up with great force so that it seemed that a storm might be in the offing and the captain ordered all sails on so that he could run before the storm and get into Behruk with all possible speed.

Hawkmoon suspected that the captain's haste had more to do with his wish to unload his passengers than his cargo, but he sympathised with the man. Another captain, after such an incident, might have been justified in throwing the remaining four overboard.

Hawkmoon's hatred for Kalan of Vitall grew more intense. This was the second time that he had been robbed of his friend by a Dark Empire lord and, if anything, he felt this second loss more painfully than he did the first, for all that he had been, in some ways, more prepared for it. He became determined, no matter what befell, to seek out Kalan and destroy him.

Disembarking on the white quayside of Behruk, the four took fewer precautions to hide their identities here. Their legends were familiar to the folk who dwelt along the Arabian Sea but their descriptions were not so well-known. None the less they lost no time in going speedily to the market-place and there purchasing four sturdy camels for their expedition into the hinterland.

Four days riding saw them used to the lolloping beasts and most of their aches gone. Four days riding also saw them on the edge of the Syranian desert, following the Euphrates as it wound through great sanddunes, while Hawkmoon looked often at the map and wished that Oladahn, the Oladahn who had fought at his side against D'Averc in Soryandum, when they were still enemies, was here to help him recall their route.

The huge, hot sun had turned Count Brass's armour into glaring gold. He dazzled the eyes of his companions almost as much as the pyramid of Kalan of Vitall had dazzled them. And Dorian Hawkmoon's steel armour shone, in contrast, like silver. Bowgentle and Huillam D'Averc, who wore no armour at all, made one or two acid comments about this effect, though he stopped when it became evident that the armoured men were suffering considerably more discomfort in the heat and, while waterholes and the river were close, took to pouring whole helmets-full of water through the necks of their breastplates.

The fifth day's riding saw them passed beyond the river and into the desert proper. Dull yellow sand stretched in all directions. It rippled sometimes, when a faint breeze blew across the desert, reminding them, intolerably, of the water they had left behind.

The sixth day's riding saw them leaning wearily over the pommels of their high saddles, their eyes glazed and their lips cracked as they preserved their water, not knowing when next they might find a waterhole.

The seventh day's riding saw Bowgentle fall from his saddle and lie spreadeagled upon the sand and it took half their remaining water to revive him. After he had fallen they sought the scant shade of a dune and remained there through the night until the next morning when Hawkmoon dragged himself to his feet and said he would continue alone.

"Alone? Why is that?" Count Brass got up, the straps of his brass armour were creaking. "For what reason, Duke of Köln?"

"I will scout while you rest. I could swear that Soryandum was near here. I will circle about until I find it—or find the site on which it stood. Whatever else, there is bound to be a source of water there."

"I can see sense in that," Count Brass agreed. "And if you grow weary, then one of us can relieve you, and so on. Are you certain that we are close to Soryandum?"

"I am. I shall look for the hills which mark the end of the desert. They should be near. If only these dunes were not so high, I am sure we should see the hills by now."

"Very well," said Count Brass. "We shall wait."

And Hawkmoon goaded his camel to its feet and rode away from where his friends still sat.

But it was not until the afternoon that he climbed the twentieth dune of the day and saw at last the green foothills of the mountains at the foot of which had lain Soryandum.

But he could not see the ruined city of the Wraith-folk. He had marked his way carefully on his map and now he retraced his journey.

He was almost back at the spot where he had left his friends when he saw the pyramid again. Foolishly he had decided to leave his encumbering flame-lances behind and he was not sure if any of the others knew how to work the lances, or whether they would care to, after what had happened to Oladahn.

He dismounted from the camel and proceeded as cautiously as he could, using the little cover available to him. Automatically he had drawn his sword.

Now words reached him from the pyramid. Kalan of Vitall was once again trying to convince his three friends that they should kill him when he returned.

"He is your enemy. Whatever else I might have told you, I spoke truth when I said that he will lead you to your deaths. You know Huillam D'Averc that you are a friend of Granbretan—Hawkmoon will turn you against the Dark Empire. And you, Bowgentle, you hate violence—Hawkmoon will make you a man of violence. And you, Count Brass, who has always been neutral where the affairs of Granbretan are concerned, he will set you upon a course which will make you fight against that very force which now you regard as a unifying factor in the future of Europe. And, as well as being deceived into acting against your better interests, you will be slain. Kill Hawkmoon now and . . ."

"Kill me, then!" Hawkmoon stood up, impatient with Kalan's cunning. "Kill me yourself, Kalan. Why can't you?"

The pyramid continued to hover over the heads of the three men as Hawkmoon looked down upon it from the dune.

"And why would killing me now make all that has gone before different, Kalan? Your logic is either very bad, or else you have not told us all that you should!"

"You grow boring, besides," said Huillam D'Averc. He drew his slim sword from its scabbard. "And I am very thirsty and tired, Baron Kalan. I think I will try my luck against you, for there's precious little else to do in this desert!"

And suddenly he had leaped forward, stabbing and stabbing again with his foil, the steel passing into the white material of the pyramid.

Kalan screamed as if wounded. "Look to your own

interest, D'Averc—it lies with me!"

D'Averc laughed and passed his sword again into the pyramid.

And again Kalan shouted. "I warn you, D'Averc—if you make me, I shall rid this world of you!"

"This world has nothing to offer. And it does not want me haunting it, either. I think I'll find your heart, Baron Kalan, if I continue to search."

He stabbed once more.

Kalan shouted once more.

Hawkmoon cried: "D'Averc, be careful!" He began to run and slide down the dune, trying to reach the flame-lance. But D'Averc had vanished, silently, before he had got halfway to the weapon.

"D'Averc!" Hawkmoon's voice had a baying quality, a mournful quality. "D'Averc!"

"Be silent, Hawkmoon," said Kalan's voice from the glowing pyramid. "Listen to me, you others. Kill him now— or D'Averc's fate shall be yours."

"It does not seem a particularly terrible fate." Count Brass smiled.

Hawkmoon picked up the flame-lance. Kalan could obviously see through the pyramid for he screamed. "Oh, you are crude, Hawkmoon. But you shall die yet."

And the pyramid faded and was gone.

Count Brass looked about him, a sardonic expression on his bronzed face. "Should we find Soryandum," he said, "it could come to pass that there'll be nothing of us to find in Soryandum. Our ranks are reducing swiftly, friend Hawkmoon."

Hawkmoon gave a deep sigh. "To lose good friends twice over is hard to bear. You cannot understand that. Oladahn and D'Averc were strangers to you as was I a stranger to them. But they were old, dear friends to me."

Bowgentle put a hand on Hawkmoon's shoulder. "I can

understand," he said. "This business is harder on you than it is on us, Duke Dorian. For all that we are bewildered—tugged from our times, given omens of death on all sides, discovering peculiar machines which order us to kill strangers—you are sad. And grief could be called the most weakening of all the emotions. It robs you of will when you most need your will."

"Aye," Hawkmoon sighed again. He flung down the flame-lance. "Well," he said. "I have found Soryandum—or, at least, the hills in which Soryandum lies. We can get there by nightfall, I'd guess."

"Then let us hurry on to Soryandum," said Count Brass. He brushed sand from his face and his moustache. "With luck we shall not see Baron Kalan and his damned pyramid for a few days yet. And by that time we might have gone a stage or two further towards solving this mystery." He slapped Hawkmoon on the back. "Come, lad. Mount up. You never know—perhaps this will all end well. Perhaps you'll see your other friends again."

Hawkmoon smiled bitterly. "I have the feeling I'll be lucky if I ever see my wife and children again, Count Brass."

chapter four

A FURTHER ENCOUNTER WITH ANOTHER OLD ENEMY

But there was no Soryandum in the green foothills bordering the Syranian desert. They found water. They found the outline which marked the area of the city, but the city had gone. Hawkmoon had seen it go, when threatened by the Dark Empire. Plainly the people of Soryandum had been wise, judging that the threat was not yet over. Wiser, Hawkmoon thought sardonically, than he. So, after all, their journey had been for nothing. There was only one other faint hope—that the cave of machines from which, years before, he had taken the crystal machines, was still intact. Miserably he led his two companions deep into the hills until Soryandum was several miles behind them.

"It seems that I have led you on a useless quest, my friends," Hawkmoon told Bowgentle and Count Brass. "And, moreover, offered you a false hope."

"Perhaps not," said Bowgentle thoughtfully. "It could be

that the machines remain intact and that I, who have some slight experience of such things, might be able to see a use for them."

Count Brass was ahead of the other two, striding in his armour of brass, up the steep hill to stand on the brow and peer into the valley below.

"Is this your cave?" he called.

Hawkmoon and Bowgentle joined him. "Aye—that's the cliff," said Hawkmoon. A cliff which looked as if a giant sword had sheared a hill in two. And there, some distance to the south, he saw the cairn of granite, made from the stone sliced from the hill to make the cave in which the weapons were stored. And there was the cave opening, a narrow slit in the cliff face. It looked undisturbed. Hawkmoon's spirits began to rise a little.

He went faster down the hill. "Come, then," he called, "let's hope the treasures are intact!"

But there was something that Hawkmoon had forgotten in his confusion of thoughts and emotions. He had forgotten that the ancient technology of the Wraith-folk had had a guardian. A guardian that he and Oladahn had fought once before and had failed to destroy. A guardian that D'Averc had only just managed to escape from. A guardian that could not be reasoned with. And Hawkmoon wished that they had not left their camels resting at the sight of Soryandum, for all he wished for now was a chance to flee swiftly.

"What is that sound?" asked Count Brass as a peculiar, muted wailing came from the crack in the cliff. "Do you recognise it, Hawkmoon?"

"Aye," said Hawkmoon miserably. "I recognise it. It is the cry of the machine-beast—the mechanical creature which guards the caves. I had assumed it destroyed but now it will destroy us, I fear."

"We have swords," said Count Brass.

Hawkmoon laughed wildly. "We have swords, aye!"

"And there are three of us," Bowgentle pointed out. "All cunning men."

"Aye."

The wailing increased as the beast scented them.

"We have only one advantage, however," said Hawkmoon softly. "The beast is blind. Our only chance is to scatter and run, making for Soryandum and our camels. There my flame-lance might prove effective for a short while."

"Run?" Count Brass looked disgruntled. He drew his great sword and stroked his red moustache. "I have never fought a mechanical beast before. I do not care to run, Hawkmoon."

"Then die—perhaps for the third time!" Hawkmoon shouted in frustration. "Listen to me Count Brass—you know I am not a coward—if we are to survive, we must get back to our camels before the beast catches us. Look!"

And the blind machine-beast emerged from the opening in the cliff, its huge head casting about for the source of the sounds and the scents it hated.

"Nion!" hissed Count Brass. "It is a large beast."

It was at least twice the size of Count Brass. Down the length of its back was a row of razor-sharp horns. Its metal scales were multicoloured and half-blinded them as it began to hop towards them. It had short hind-legs and long fore-legs which ended in metal talons. Roughly of the proportions of a large gorilla, it had multi-faceted eyes which had been broken in a previous fight with Hawkmoon and Oladahn. As it moved, it clashed. Its voice was metallic and made their teeth ache. Its smell, coming to them even from that distance, was also metallic.

Hawkmoon tugged at Count Brass's arm. "Please, Count Brass, I beg you. This is not the right ground on which to choose to make a stand."

This logic appealed to Count Brass. "Aye," he said, "I

can see that. Very well, we'll make for the flat ground again. Will it follow us?"

"Oh, of that you can be certain!"

And then, in three slightly different directions, the companions began to run back towards the site of Soryandum as fast as they could before the beast decided which of them it would follow.

Their camels could smell the machine-beast, that was evident as they came panting back to where they had tethered their animals. The camels were tugging at the ropes which had been pegged to the ground. Their ugly heads reared, their mouths and nostrils twisted, their eyes rolled and their hooves thumped nervously at the barren ground.

Again the wailing shriek of the machine-beast echoed through the hills behind them.

Hawkmoon handed a flame-lance to Count Brass, "I doubt if these will have much effect, but we must try them."

Count Brass grumbled. "I'd have preferred a hand to hand engagement with the thing."

"That could still happen," Hawkmoon told him with grim humour.

Hopping, waddling, running on all fours, the mighty metal beast emerged over the nearest hill, pausing as, again, it sought their scent—perhaps it even heard the sound of their heartbeats.

Bowgentle positioned himself behind his friends, for he had no flame-lance. "I am beginning to become tired of dying," he said with a smile. "Is that the fate of the dead, then? To die again and again through uncountable incarnations? It is not an appealing conception."

"Now!" Hawkmoon said, and pressed the stud of his flame-lance. At the same time Count Brass activated his lance.

Ruby fire struck the mechanical beast and it snorted. Its scales glowed and in places became white hot, but the heat did not seem to have any effect upon the beast at all. It did not notice the flame-lances. Shaking his head, Hawkmoon switched off his lance and Count Brass did the same. It would be stupid to use up the lances' power.

"There is only one way to deal with such a monster," said Count Brass.

"And what is that?"

"It would have to be lured into a pit..."

"But we do not have a pit," Bowgentle pointed out, nervously eyeing the creature as it began to hop nearer.

"Or a cliff," said Count Brass. "If it could be tricked to fall over a cliff..."

"There is no cliff near by," Bowgentle said patiently.

"Then we shall perish, I suppose," said Count Brass with a shrug of his brazen shoulders. And then, before they could guess at what he planned, he had drawn his great broadsword and with a wild battle-yell was rushing upon the machine-beast—seemingly a man of metal attacking a monster of metal.

The monster roared. It stopped and it reared upon its hindquarters, its taloned paws slashing here and there at random, making the very air whistle.

Count Brass ducked beneath the claws and aimed a blow at the thing's midriff. His sword clanged on its scales and clanged again. Then Count Brass had jumped back, out of the reach of those slashing talons, bringing his sword down upon the great wrist as it passed him.

Hawkmoon joined him now, battering at one of the creature's legs with his own sword. And Bowgentle, able to forget his dislike of killing where this mechanical thing was concerned, tried to drive his blade up into the machine-beast's face, only to have the metal jaws close on the sword and snap it off cleanly.

"Get back, Bowgentle," Hawkmoon said. "You can do nothing now."

And the beast's head turned at the sound and the talons slashed again so that, in avoiding them, Hawkmoon stumbled and fell.

In again came Count Brass, roaring almost as loudly as his adversary. Again the blade clanged on the scales. And again the beast turned to seek the source of this new irritation.

But all three were tiring. Their journeys across the desert had weakened them. Their run from the hills had tired them further. Hawkmoon knew that it was inevitable that they should perish here in the desert and that none should know the manner of their passing.

He saw Count Brass shout as he was flung backwards several feet by a sideswipe of the beast's paw. The Count, encumbered by his heavy armour, fell helplessly upon the barren ground, winded and, for the moment, unable to rise.

The metal beast sensed its opponent's weakness and lumbered forward to crush Count Brass beneath its huge feet.

Hawkmoon shouted wordlessly and ran at the thing, bringing his sword down upon its back. But it did not pause. Closer and closer it came to where Count Brass lay.

Hawkmoon darted around to put himself between the creature and his friend. He struck at its whirling talons, at its torso. His bones ached horribly as his sword shuddered with every blow he struck.

And still the beast refused to alter its course, its blind eyes staring ahead of it.

Then Hawkmoon, too, was flung aside and lay bruised and dazed, watching in horror as Count Brass struggled to rise. He saw one of the monstrous feet rise up above Count Brass's head, saw Count Brass raise an arm as if it would protect him from being crushed. Somehow he managed to get to his feet and began to stumble forward, knowing that he would be too late to save Count Brass, even if he could get to the machine-beast in time. And as he moved, so did

Bowgentle—Bowgentle who had no weapon save the stump of a sword—rushing at the beast as if he thought he could turn it aside with his bare hands.

And Hawkmoon thought: "I have brought my friends to yet another death. It is true what Kalan told them. I am their nemesis, it seems."

chapter five

SOME OTHER LONDRA

And then the metal beast hesitated.

It whined almost plaintively.

Count Brass was not one to miss such an opportunity. Swiftly he rolled from under the great foot. He still did not have the strength to rise to his feet, but he began to crawl away, his sword still in his hand.

Both Bowgentle and Hawkmoon paused, wondering what had caused the beast to stop.

The machine-creature cringed. Its whine became placatory, fearful. It turned its head on one side as if it heard a voice which none of the others could hear.

Count Brass rose, at last, to his feet and wearily prepared himself again to fight the monster.

Then, with an enormous crash which made the earth shake, the beast fell and the bright colours of its scales became dull as if suddenly rusted. It did not move.

"What?" Count Brass's deep voice was puzzled. "Did we *will* it to death?"

Hawkmoon began to laugh as he noticed the faintest of outlines begin to appear against the clear, desert sky. "Someone might have done," he said.

Bowgentle gasped as he, too, noticed the outlines. "What is it? The ghost of a city?"

"Almost."

Count Brass growled. He sniffed and hefted his sword. "I like this new danger no better."

"It should not be a danger—to us," said Hawkmoon. "Soryandum is returning."

Slowly they saw the outlines grow firmer until soon a whole city lay spread across the desert. An ancient city. A ruined city.

Count Brass cursed and stroked his red moustache, his stance still that of one prepared for an attack.

"Sheath your sword, Count Brass," Hawkmoon said. "This is Soryandum that we sought. The Wraith-folk, those ancient immortals of whom I told you, have come to our rescue. This is lovely Soryandum. Look."

And Soryandum was lovely, for all that she lay in ruins. Her moss-grown walls, her fountains, her tall, broken towers, her blossoms of ochre, orange and purple, her cracked, marble pavements, her columns of granite and obsidian— all were beautiful. And there was an air of tranquillity about the city, even about the birds which nested in her time-worn houses, the dust which blew through her deserted streets.

"This is Soryandum," said Hawkmoon again, almost in a whisper.

They stood in a square, beside the dead beast of metal.

Count Brass was the first to move, crossing the weed-grown pavement and touching a column. "It is solid enough," he grunted. "How can this be?"

"I have ever rejected the more sensational claims of those

who believe in the supernatural," said Bowgentle. "But now I begin to wonder..."

"This is science that has brought Soryandum here," Hawkmoon said. "And it is science that took her away. I know. I supplied the machine the Wraith-folk needed, for it is impossible for them to leave their city now. These folk were like us once, but over the centuries, according to a process I cannot begin to understand, they have rid themselves of physical form and have become creatures of mind alone. They can take physical shape when they desire it and they have greater strength than most mortals. They are a peaceful people—and as beautiful as this city of theirs."

"You are most flattering, old friend," said a voice from the air.

"Rinal?" said Hawkmoon, recognising the voice. "Is that you?"

"It is I. But who are your companions? Our instruments are confused by them. It is for this reason that we were reluctant to reveal either ourselves or our city, in case they should have deceived you in some way into leading them to Soryandum when they had evil designs against our city."

"They are good friends," said Hawkmoon, "but not of this time. Is that what confuses your instruments, Rinal?"

"It could be. Well, I shall trust you Hawkmoon, for I have reason to. You are a welcome guest in Soryandum, for it is thanks to you that we still survive."

"And it is thanks to you that I survive." Hawkmoon smiled. "Where are you Rinal?"

The figure of Rinal, tall, ethereal, appeared suddenly beside him. His body was naked and without ornament and it had a kind of milky opaque quality. His face was thin and his eyes seemed blind—as blind as those of the machine-beast—yet looked clearly at Hawkmoon.

"Ghosts of cities, ghosts of men," said Count Brass sheathing his sword. "Still, if you saved our lives from that thing," he pointed at the dead machine-beast, "I must thank you." He recovered his grace and bowed. "I thank you most humbly, Sir Ghost."

"I regret that our beast caused you so much trouble," said Rinal of Soryandum. "We created it to protect our treasures, many centuries ago. We would have destroyed it, save that we feared the Dark Empire folk would return to take our machines and put them to evil use—and also, we could do nothing until it came into the environs of our city, for, as you know, Dorian Hawkmoon, we have no power beyond Soryandum now. Our existence is completely linked with the existence of the city. It was an easy matter to tell the beast to die, however, once it was here."

"It was as well for us, Duke Dorian, that you advised us to flee back here," said Bowgentle feelingly. "Otherwise we should all three be dead by now."

"Where is your other friend," said Rinal. "The one who came with you first to Soryandum!"

"Oladahn is twice-dead," said Hawkmoon in a low voice.

"Twice?"

"Aye—just as these other friends of mine came close to dying for at least a second time."

"You intrigue me," said Rinal. "Come, we'll find you something with which to sustain yourselves as you explain all these mysteries to myself and the few others of my folk who remain."

Rinal led the three companions through the broken streets of Soryandum until they came to a three-storied house which had no entrance at ground level. Hawkmoon had visited the house before. Although superficially no different to the other ruins of Soryandum, this was where the Wraith-folk lived when they needed to take material form.

And now two others emerged from above, drifting down towards Hawkmoon, Count Brass and Bowgentle and lifting them effortlessly, bearing them upward to the second level and a wide window which was the entrance to the house.

In a bare, clean room food was brought to them, though Rinal's folk had no need of food themselves. The food was delicious, though unfamiliar. Count Brass attacked it with vigour, speaking hardly at all as he listened to Hawkmoon tell Rinal of why they sought the assistance of the Wraith-folk of Soryandum.

And when Hawkmoon had finished his tale, Count Brass continued to eat, to Bowgentle's quiet amusement. Bowgentle himself was more interested in learning more about Soryandum and its inhabitants, its history and its science and Rinal told him much, between listening to Hawkmoon. He told Bowgentle how, during the Tragic Millennium, most of the great cities and nations had concentrated their energies on producing more and more powerful weapons of war. But Soryandum had been able to remain neutral, thanks to her remote geographical position. She had concentrated on understanding more of the nature of space, of matter and of time. Thus she had survived the Tragic Millennium and remembered all her knowledge while elsewhere knowledge died and superstition replaced it, as was ever the case in such situations.

"And that is why we now seek your help," said Hawkmoon. "We wish to find out how Baron Kalan escaped and to where he fled. We wish to discover how he manages to manipulate the stuff of time, to bring Count Brass and Bowgentle—and the others I mentioned—from one age to another and still not create a paradox in our minds at least."

"That sounds the simplest of the problems," said Rinal. "This Kalan seems to have got control of enormous power. Is he the one who destroyed your crystal machine—the one we gave you which allowed you to shift your own castle and city out of this space-time?"

"No, that was Taragorm I believe," Hawkmoon told Rinal. "But Kalan is just as clever as the old Master of the Palace of Time. However, I suspect that he is unsure of the nature of his power. He is reluctant to test it to its fullest extent. And, also, he seems to think that my death *now* might change *past* history. Is that possible?"

Rinal looked thoughtful. "It could be," he said. "This Baron Kalan must have a very subtle understanding of time. Objectively, of course, there is no such thing as past, present or future. Yet Baron Kalan's plot seems unnecessarily complicated. If he can manipulate time to that extent, could he not merely seek to destroy you *before*—subjectively speaking—you could be of service to the Runestaff?"

"That would change all the events concerning our defeat of the Dark Empire?"

"That is one of the paradoxes. Events are events. They occur. They are truth. But truth varies in different dimensions. It is just possible that there is some dimension of Earth so like your own that similar events are about to take place in it . . ." Rinal smiled. Count Brass's bronzed forehead had furrowed and he was plucking at his moustache and shaking his head from side to side as if he thought Rinal mad.

"You have another suggestion, Count Brass?"

"Politics are my interest," said Count Brass. "I've never cared overmuch for the more abstract areas of philosophy. My mind is not trained to follow your reasoning."

Hawkmoon laughed. "Mine, neither. Only Bowgentle appears to know of what Rinal speaks."

"Something," Bowgentle admitted. "Something. You think that Kalan might be in some other dimension of the Earth where a Count Brass, say, exists who is not quite the same as the Count Brass who sits beside me now?"

"What?" Count Brass growled. "Have I a doppelganger?"

Hawkmoon laughed again. But Bowgentle's face was serious as he said: "Not quite, Count Brass. It occurs to me that, in this world, you would be the doppelganger—and I, for that matter. I believe that this is not our world—that the past we recall would not be quite the same, in detail, as that which friend Hawkmoon recalls. We are interlopers, through no fault of our own. Brought here to kill Duke Dorian. Yet, save for reasons of perverse vengeance, why could not Baron Kalan kill Duke Dorian himself? Why must he use us?"

"Because of the repercussions—if your theory is correct—" put in Rinal. "His action must conflict with some other action which is against his interests. If he slays Hawkmoon, something will happen to him—a chain of events will come to pass which would be just that much different to the chain of events which will take place if one of you kills him."

"Yet he must have allowed for the possibility that we would not be deceived into killing Hawkmoon?"

"I think not," said Rinal. "I think things have gone awry for Baron Kalan. That is why he continued to try to force you to kill Hawkmoon even when it became obvious that you were suspicious of the situation. He must have based some plan on the expectation of Hawkmoon's being slain in the Kamarg. That is why he grows more and more hysterical. Doubtless he has other schemes afoot and sees them all endangered by Hawkmoon's continuing to live. That, too, is why he has only dispatched those of you who have directly attacked him. He is somehow vulnerable. You would be well advised to discover the nature of that vulnerability."

Hawkmoon shrugged. "What chance have we of making such a discovery, when we do not even know where Baron Kalan is hiding?"

"It might be possible to find him," mused Rinal. "There are certain devices we invented when we were learning to shift our city through the dimensions—sensors and the like which can probe the various layers of the multiverse. We shall have to prepare them. We have used only one probe, to watch this area of our own Earth while we remained hidden in the other dimension. To activate the others will take a short while. Would this be helpful to you?"

"It would," said Hawkmoon.

"Does it mean we'll be given a chance to get our hands on Kalan?" growled Count Brass.

Bowgentle placed a hand on the shoulder of the man who would become, in later years, his closest friend. "You are impetuous, Count. Rinal's machines can only see into these dimensions. It will be another matter altogether, I am sure, to travel into them."

Rinal inclined his thin-skulled head. "That is true. However, let us see if we *can* find Baron Kalan of the Dark Empire. There is a good chance that we shall fail—for there are an infinity of dimensions, of this Earth alone."

Through most of the following day, while Rinal and his people worked on their machines, Hawkmoon, Bowgentle and Count Brass slept, recouping the strength they had expended in travelling to Soryandum and fighting the metal beast.

And then, in the evening, Rinal floated through the window so that the rays of the setting sun seemed to radiate from his opaque body.

"They are ready, the devices," he said. "Will you come now? We are beginning to scan the dimensions."

Count Brass leapt up. "Aye, we'll come."

The others rose as two of Rinal's fellows entered the room and, in strong arms, lifted them up, through the window and to the floor above where were assembled an array of machines unlike any machines they had ever seen before. Like the crystal device which had shifted Castle Brass through the dimensions, these were more like jewels than machines—some of the jewels nearly the height of a man. At each of the machines floated one of the Wraith-folk, manipulating smaller jewels, not dissimilar to that small pyramid which Hawkmoon had seen in the hands of Baron Kalan.

A thousand pictures flashed upon the screens as the probes delved the dimensions of the multiverse, showing peculiar, alien scenes, many of which seemed to bear little relation to any Earth Hawkmoon knew.

And then, hours later, Hawkmoon cried: "There! A beast-mask! I saw it."

The operator stroked a series of crystals, trying to fix on the image which had flashed on to the screen so briefly. But it was gone.

Again the probes began their search. Twice more Hawkmoon thought he saw scenes providing evidence of Kalan's whereabouts, but twice more they lost the scene.

And then, at last, by the purest chance, they saw a white, glowing pyramid and it was unmistakably the pyramid in which Baron Kalan travelled.

The sensors received a particularly strong signal, for the pyramid was in the process of completing a journey of its own, returning, Hawkmoon hoped, to its base.

"We can follow it easily enough. Watch."

Hawkmoon, Count Brass and Bowgentle gathered round the screen as it shadowed the milky pyramid until at last it came to a stop and began to turn transparent, revealing the hateful face of Baron Kalan of Vitall. Unaware that he was being observed by those he sought to destroy, he climbed from his pyramid into a large, dark, untidy room that might have been a copy of his old laboratory in Londra. He was frowning, consulting notes he had made. Another figure appeared and spoke to him, though the three friends heard no sound. The figure was clad in the old manner of the folk of the Dark Empire—a huge, cumbersome mask was on his head, completely covering it. The mask was of metal, enamelled in a score of colours, and had been fashioned to resemble the head of a hissing serpent.

Hawkmoon recognised it as the mask of the Order of the Snake—the order to which all sorcerers and scientists of old Granbretan had had to belong. Even as they watched, the snake-masked one handed another mask to Kalan who donned it hurriedly, for no Granbretanian of his kind could bear to be seen unmasked by any of his fellows.

Kalan's mask was also in the form of a serpent's head, but more ornate than his servant's.

Hawkmoon rubbed at his jaw, wondering why he felt something was wrong about the scene. He wished that D'Averc, more familiar with the intimate ways of the Dark Empire, was with him now, for D'Averc would have noticed.

And then it dawned on Hawkmoon that these masks were cruder than any he had seen in Londra, even those worn by the humblest servants. The finish of the masks, their design, was not of the same quality. But why should this be?

Now the probes followed Kalan from his laboratory and through winding passages very like those which had once connected buildings in Londra. Superficially this place could have been Londra. But, again, these passages were subtly different. The stone was poorly faced, the carvings and murals were by inferior artists. None of this would have been tolerated in Londra where, for all their perverse tastes, the Lords of the Dark Empire had demanded the highest standards of craftsmanship, down to the smallest detail.

Here, detail was lacking. The whole thing resembled a bad copy of a painting.

The scene flickered as Kalan entered another chamber where more masked ones met. This chamber also looked familiar, but crude, like everything else.

Count Brass was fuming. "When can we get there? That's our enemy. Let's deal with him at once!"

"It is not easy to travel through the dimensions," Rinal said mildly. "Moreover, we have not yet traced exactly where it is that we were watching."

Hawkmoon smiled at Count Brass. "Have patience, sir."

This Count Brass was more impetuous than the man Hawkmoon had known. Doubtless it was because he was some twenty years younger. Or perhaps, as Rinal had suggested, he was not the same man—only a man very nearly the same, from another dimension. Still, Hawkmoon thought, he was satisfied with this Count Brass, wherever he came from.

"Our probe falters," said the Wraith-man operating the screen. "The dimension we study must be many layers away."

Rinal nodded. "Aye, many. Somewhere even our old adventuring ancestors never explored. It will be hard to find a doorway through."

"Kalan found one," Hawkmoon pointed out.

Rinal smiled faintly. "By accident or by design, friend Hawkmoon?"

"By design, surely? Where else would he have discovered some other Londra?"

"New cities can be built," said Rinal.

"Aye," said Bowgentle. "And so can new realities."

chapter six

ANOTHER VICTIM

The three men waited anxiously while Rinal and his people considered the possibility of journeying into the dimension where Baron Kalan of Vitall was hiding.

"Since this new cult has grown up in the real Londra, I would assume that Kalan is visiting his supporters secretly. That explains the rumour that some of the Dark Empire Lords are still alive in Londra," Hawkmoon mused. "Our only other chance would be to go to Londra and seek Kalan out there, when he makes his next visit. But would we have the time?"

Count Brass shook his head. "That Kalan—he is desperate to accomplish his scheme. Why he should be so hysterical, with all the dimensions of space and time to play with, I cannot guess. Yet, though he can presumably manipulate us at will, he does not. I wonder why we should be so crucial to his plans?"

Hawkmoon shrugged. "Perhaps we are not. He would

not be the first Dark Empire Lord to let a thirst for vengeance get in the way of his own self-interest." He told them the story of Baron Meliadus.

Bowgentle had been pacing among the crystalline instruments, trying to understand the principles by which they worked, but they defeated him. Now they were all dormant as the Wraith-folk busied themselves in another part of the building with the problem of designing a machine which could shift through the dimensions. They would adapt the crystal engine which moved their city, but the actual engine they must retain, in case further danger threatened them.

"Well," said Bowgentle, scratching his head, "I can make nothing of the things. All I can say for certain is that they work!"

Count Brass stirred in his armour. He went to the window and looked out into cool night. "I'm becoming impatient with being cooped up here," he said. "I could do with some fresh air. What about you two?"

Hawkmoon shook his head. "I'll rest."

"I'll come with you," said Bowgentle to Count Brass. "But how do we leave?"

"Call Rinal," Hawkmoon said. "He'll hear you."

And this they did, looking slightly uncomfortable as the Wraith-folk, seemingly so frail, bore them through the window and down to the earth. Hawkmoon settled himself in a corner of the room and slept.

But strange, disquieting dreams, in which his friends changed into enemies and his enemies into friends, the living became the dead and the dead became the living, while some became the unborn, disturbed him and he forced himself awake, sweating, to find Rinal standing over him.

"The machine is ready," said the Wraith-man. "But it is not perfect, I fear. All it can do is pursue your pyramid. Once the pyramid materialises in this world again, our sphere will follow it, wherever it goes—but it has no navigating power of its own—it can *only* follow the pyramid. Therefore there is a strong danger of your being trapped in some other dimension for all time."

"It is a risk I'm prepared to take, for one," Hawkmoon said. "It will be better than the nightmares I experience, awake or dreaming. Where are Count Brass and Bowgentle?"

"Somewhere near by, walking and talking through the streets of Soryandum. Shall I tell them you wish to see them?"

"Aye," said Hawkmoon, rubbing sleep from his eyes. "We had best make our plans as soon as possible. I have a feeling we shall see Kalan again before long." He stretched and yawned. The sleep had not really helped him. Rather it appeared to have made him feel wearier than before.

He changed his mind. "No, perhaps I had better speak with them myself. The air might refresh me."

"As you will. I'll take you down." Rinal floated towards Hawkmoon.

As Rinal began to lift him towards the window, Hawkmoon asked: "Where is the machine you mentioned?"

"The dimension-travelling sphere? Below in our laboratory. Would you like to see it tonight?"

"I think I had better. I have a feeling Kalan could reappear at any time."

"Very well. I shall bring it to you shortly. The controls are simple—indeed they are scarcely controls at all since the purpose of the sphere is to make itself the slave of another machine. However, I understand your eagerness to see it. Go now and speak with your friends."

The Wraith-man, virtually invisible in the moonlit street, drifted away, leaving Hawkmoon to find Bowgentle and Count Brass by himself.

He walked through overgrown streets, between ruined

buildings through which the moonlight glared, enjoying the peace of the night and feeling his head begin to clear. The air was very sweet and cool.

At length he heard voices ahead of him and was about to call out when he realised that he heard the tones of three voices, not two. He began to run softly towards the source of the voices, keeping to the shadows, until he stood in the cover of a ruined colonnade and looked into a small square where stood Count Brass and Bowgentle. Count Brass stood frozen, as if mesmerised, and Bowgentle was remonstrating in a low voice with a man who sat cross-legged in the air above him, the outline of the pyramid glowing only very faintly, as if Kalan had deliberately tried to escape attention. Kalan was glaring at Bowgentle.

"What do you know of such matters?" Baron Kalan demanded. "Why—you are barely real yourself!"

"That's as may be. I suspect that your own reality is also at stake, is it not? Why can you not kill Hawkmoon yourself? Because of the repercussions, eh? Have you plotted the possibilities following such an action? Are they not very palatable?"

"Be silent, puppet!" Baron Kalan demanded. "Or you, too, will return to limbo. I offer you full life if you destroy Hawkmoon—or can convince Count Brass to do it!"

"Why did you not send Count Brass to limbo just now when he attacked you? Is it because you must have Hawkmoon killed by one of us and now there are only two left who can do your work?"

"I told you to be silent!" Kalan snarled. "You should have worked with the Dark Empire, Sir Bowgentle. Such wit as yours is wasted among the barbarians."

Bowgentle smiled. "Barbarians? I have heard something of what, in my future, the Dark Empire will do to its enemies. Your choice of words is poor, Baron Kalan."

"I warned you," Kalan said menacingly. "You go too far. I am still a Lord of Granbretan. I cannot tolerate such familiarity! '

"Your lack of tolerance has been your downfall once— or will be. We are beginning to understand what it is you try to do in your imitation Londra..."

"You know?" Kalan looked almost frightened. His lips pursed and his brows drew together. "You know, eh? I think we made a mistake in bringing a pawn of your perception on to the board, Sir Bowgentle."

"Aye, perhaps you did."

Kalan began to fiddle with the small pyramid he held in his hand. "Then it would be wise to sacrifice that pawn now," he muttered.

Bowgentle seemed to realise what was in Kalan's mind. He took a step backward. "Is that really wise? Are you not manipulating forces you barely understand?"

"Perhaps." Baron Kalan chuckled. "But that is no comfort to you, eh?"

Bowgentle grew pale.

Hawkmoon made to move forward, wondering at the manner in which Count Brass still remained frozen, seemingly unaware of what was taking place. Then he felt a light touch on his shoulder and he started, turning and reaching for his sword. But it was the almost invisible Wraith-man, Rinal, who stood behind him. Rinal whispered:

"The sphere comes. This is your chance to follow the pyramid."

"But Bowgentle is in danger..." Hawkmoon murmured. "I must try to save him."

"You will not be able to save him. It is unlikely that he will be harmed, that he will retain anything but the dimmest memory of these events—as you recall a fading dream."

"But he is my friend..."

"You will serve him better if you can find a way of

stopping Kalan's activities for ever." Rinal pointed. Several of his folk were drifting down the street towards them. They were carrying a large sphere of glowing yellow. "There will be a few moments after the pyramid has gone when you'll be able to follow it."

"But Count Brass—he has been mesmerised by Kalan."

"The power will fade when Kalan leaves."

Bowgentle was speaking hurriedly. "Why should you fear my knowledge, Baron Kalan? You are strong. I am weak. It is you who manipulates me!"

"The more you know the less I can predict," said Kalan. "It is simple, Sir Bowgentle. Farewell."

And Bowgentle cried out, whirled as if trying to escape. He began to run and as he ran he faded, faded until he had disappeared altogether.

Hawkmoon heard Baron Kalan laugh. It was a familiar laugh. A laugh he had grown to hate. Only Rinal's hand on his shoulder stopped him from attacking Kalan who, still unaware that he was observed, addressed Count Brass:

"You will gain much, Count Brass, by serving my purpose—and gain nothing if you do not. Why should it be Hawkmoon who plagues me always? I had thought it a simple matter to eliminate him and yet in every probability I investigate he emerges again. He is eternal, I sometimes think—perhaps immortal. Only if he is slain by another hero, another champion of that damned Runestaff, can events progress along the course I choose. So slay him, Count Brass. Earn life for yourself and for me!"

Count Brass moved his head. He blinked. He looked around him as if he did not see the pyramid, or its occupant.

The pyramid began to glow with a milky whiteness. The whiteness became brilliant, blinding. Count Brass cursed and threw his arm up to protect his eyes.

And then the brilliance faded and there was only a dim outline against the night.

"Quickly," said Rinal. "Into the sphere."

As Hawkmoon passed through an entrance that was like a flimsy curtain which instantly reformed behind him, he saw Rinal drift over to Count Brass, seize him and bear him to the sphere, flinging him in after Hawkmoon so that he sprawled, sword still in hand, at Hawkmoon's feet.

"The sapphire," Rinal said urgently. "Touch the sapphire. It is all you must do. And I wish you success, Dorian Hawkmoon, in that other Londra!"

Hawkmoon reached out and touched the sapphire stone suspended in the air before him.

At once the sphere seemed to spin around them, while he and Count Brass remained motionless. They were in complete blackness now and the white pyramid could be seen through the walls of the sphere.

Suddenly there was sunshine and a landscape of green rocks. This faded almost as quickly as it had appeared. More images followed rapidly.

Megaliths of light, lakes of boiling metal, cities of glass and steel, battlefields on which thousands fought, forests through which strode shadowy giants, frozen seas—and always the pyramid was ahead of them as if shifted through plane after plane of the Earth, through worlds which seemed totally alien and worlds which seemed absolutely identical to Hawkmoon's.

Once before had Hawkmoon travelled through the dimensions. But then he had been escaping from danger. Now he went towards it.

Count Brass spoke for the first time. "What happened back there? I remember trying to attack Baron Kalan, deciding that even if he sent me to limbo I should have his life first. Next I was in this—this chariot. Where is Bowgentle?"

"Bowgentle had begun to understand Kalan's plot,"

Hawkmoon said grimly, keeping his eyes fixed on the pyramid ahead. "And so Kalan banished him back to wherever it was he came from. But Kalan also gave something away. He said that, for some reason, I could only be slain by a friend—by some other who had served the Runestaff. And that, he said, would ensure the friend's life."

Count Brass shrugged. "It still has the smell of a perverse plot to me. Why should it matter who slays you?"

"Well, Count Brass," said Hawkmoon soberly. "I have often said that I would give anything for you not to have died on the battlefield at Londra. I would give my life, even. So, if the time ever comes when you wish to be done with all this—you can always kill me."

Count Brass laughed. "If you want to die, Dorian Hawkmoon, I am sure you can find one more used to cold-blooded assassination in Londra, or wherever it is we journey to now." He sheathed his great brass-hilted sword. "I'll save my own strength for dealing with Baron Kalan and his servants when we get there!"

"If they are not prepared for us," said Hawkmoon, as wild scenes continued to come and go at even greater speed. He felt dizzy and he closed his eyes. "This journey through infinity appears to take an infinity! Once I cursed the Runestaff for meddling in my affairs, but now I wish greatly that Orland Fank was here to advise me. Still, it is plain by now that the Runestaff plays no part in this."

"Just as well," growled Count Brass. "There is already too much sorcery and science involved for my taste! I'll be happier when all this is finished, even should it mean my own death!"

Hawkmoon nodded his agreement. He was remembering Yisselda and his children, Manfred and Yarmila. He was remembering the quiet life of the Kamarg and the satisfactions he had got from seeing the marshlands restocked, the harvests brought in. And he was regretting bitterly that he had ever allowed himself to fall into the trap Baron Kalan had evidently set for him when he had sent Count Brass through time to haunt the Kamarg.

And at that, another thought occurred to him. Had *all* this been a trap?

Did Baron Kalan actually *want* to be followed? Were they being lured, even now, to their doom?

book three

OLD DREAMS
AND NEW

chapter one

THE WORLD HALF-MADE

Count Brass, lying uncomfortably along the curve of the sphere's interior, groaned and shifted his brass-clad bulk again. He peered through the misty yellow wall and watched the landscape outside change forty times in as many seconds. The pyramid was still ahead of them. Sometimes the outline of Baron Kalan could be seen within. Sometimes the vessel's surface turned to that familiar, blinding white.

"Ah, my eyes ache!" grumbled Count Brass. "They grow weary of so many variegated sights. And my head aches when I strive to consider exactly what is happening to us. If I should ever tell of this adventure I shall never have my word believed again!"

And then Hawkmoon cautioned him to silence, for the scenes came and went much more slowly until at last they ceased to change. They hung in darkness. All they could see beyond the sphere was the white pyramid.

Light came from somewhere.

Hawkmoon recognised Baron Kalan's laboratory. He acted swiftly, instinctively. "Quickly, Count Brass, we must leave the sphere."

They dived through the curtain and onto the dirty flag-stones of the floor. By chance they were behind several large and crazily shaped machines at the back of the lab-oratory.

Hawkmoon saw the sphere shudder and vanish. Now only Kalan's pyramid offered an escape from this dimen-sion. Familiar smells and sounds came to Hawkmoon. He remembered when he had first visited Kalan's laboratories, as a prisoner of Baron Meliadus, to have the Black Jewel implanted in his skull. He felt a strange coldness in his bones. Their arrival had been unnoticed it seemed, for Kalan's serpent-masked servants had their attention on the pyramid, standing ready to hand their master his own mask when he emerged. The pyramid sank slowly to the ground and Kalan stepped out of it, accepting the mask without a word and donning it. There was something hasty about his movements. He said something to his servants and they all followed him as he left the laboratory.

Cautiously Hawkmoon and Count Brass emerged. Both had unsheathed their swords.

Assured that the laboratory was, indeed, completely de-serted, they debated their next action.

"Perhaps we should wait until Kalan returns and slay him on the spot," Count Brass suggested, "using his own ma-chine for our escape."

"We do not know how to operate the machine," Hawk-moon reminded his friend. "No, I think we should learn more of this world and Kalan's plans before we consider killing him. For all we know he has other allies, more powerful than himself, who would continue to put his schemes into effect."

"That's fair enough," Count Brass agreed. "But this place

makes me nervous. I've never been one to enjoy being underground. I prefer the open spaces. That's why I could never remain in one city for long."

Hawkmoon began to inspect Baron Kalan's machines. Many of them were familiar to him in appearance, but he could make out little of their functions. He wondered if he should destroy the machines first, but then he decided it would be wiser to learn for what purpose they were intended. They could produce a disaster by tampering with the kind of forces with which Kalan was experimenting.

"With the right masks and clothes," Hawkmoon said, as they both padded towards the door, "we would have an improved chance of exploring this place undiscovered. I think we should make that objective our first priority."

Count Brass agreed.

They opened the door of the laboratory and found themselves in a low-ceilinged passage. The smell was musty, the air stale. Once the whole of Londra had reeked of the same stink. But, now that he was able to inspect the murals and carvings on the walls more closely, Hawkmoon was certain this was not Londra. The absence of detail was most noticeable. Paintings were done in outline and then filled in with solid colours, not the subtle shades of the clever Granbretanian artists. And whereas colours had been clashed in old Londra with the intention of making an effect, these colours were merely poorly selected. It was as if someone who had only seen Londra for half-an-hour or so had tried to recreate it.

Even Count Brass, who had only visited Granbretan once, on some diplomatic errand, noticed the contrast. On they crept, without encountering anyone, trying to determine which way Baron Kalan had gone, when all at once they had turned a corner in the passage and come face to face with two soldiers of the Mantis Order—King Huon's old Order—armed with long pikes and swords.

Immediately, Count Brass and Hawkmoon took up a fighting stance, expecting the two soldiers to attack. The mantis-masks nodded on the men's shoulders, but they only stared at Count Brass and his companion, as if puzzled.

One of the soldiers spoke in a vague, muffled voice from within his mantis-helm. "Why do you go unmasked?" he said. "Should this be?"

His voice had a distant, dreamlike quality, not unlike that of Count Brass when Hawkmoon had first encountered him in the Kamarg.

"Aye. It is correct," said Hawkmoon. "You are to give us your masks."

"But unmasking is forbidden in the passages!" said the second soldier in horror. His gauntleted hands went to his great-insect helm as if to protect it. Mantis eyes seemed to stare sardonically into Hawkmoon's.

"Then we must fight you for them," growled Count Brass. "Draw your swords."

Slowly the two drew their swords. Slowly they assumed defensive positions.

It was horrible work, killing those two, for they did not make any more than a token effort to defend themselves. They went down in the space of half-a-minute and Hawkmoon and Count Brass began immediately to strip them of their masks and their outer clothes of green silk and green velvet.

They stripped the pair just in time. Hawkmoon was wondering what to do with the bodies when, suddenly, they vanished.

Count Brass snorted suspiciously. "More sorcery?"

"Or an explanation of why they behaved so strangely," said Hawkmoon thoughtfully. "They vanished as Bowgentle, Oladahn and D'Averc vanished. The Mantis Order was ever the fiercest in Granbretan and those who belonged to it were arrogant, proud and quick to strike. Either those fellows were not really of Granbretan, but playing parts for Baron Kalan's benefit—or else they *were* from Granbretan, but in some kind of trance."

"They seemed to be in a dream, right enough," agreed Count Brass.

Hawkmoon adjusted his stolen mask upon his head. "Best behave the same, if challenged," he said. "That, too, will be to our advantage."

Together they continued to make their way through the passages, moving at a measured pace, like that of patrolling soldiers.

"At least," said Count Brass in a low voice, "we shall have little trouble with corpses if all those we slay disappear with such fortunate alacrity!"

They paused at several doors and tried them, but all were secured. They passed many other masked men, from all the main orders—Pig, Vulture, Dragon, Wolf and the like— but saw no other members of the Order of the Snake. Members of this Order, they were sure, would lead them eventually to Kalan. It would also be useful to exchange mantis-masks for serpent masks at some stage. Finally they found themselves at a door larger than the others and this was guarded by two men who wore the same masks now worn by Hawkmoon and Count Brass. A guarded door was an important door, thought Hawkmoon. Behind it might lie something which would help answer the questions he had followed Kalan to solve. He thought quickly, saying in as dreamy a voice as he could manage:

"We have orders to relieve you. You may return to your quarters now."

One of the guards spoke. "Relieve us? Have we been here for a full period of duty, then? I thought it was but an hour. But then time..." He paused. "It is all so strange."

"You are relieved," said Count Brass, guessing Hawkmoon's plan. "That is all we know."

Sluggishly the two guards saluted and marched away, leaving Hawkmoon and Count Brass to take up their positions.

As soon as the guards were gone, Hawkmoon turned and tried the latch of the door. It was locked.

Count Brass glanced around him, shuddering. "This seems more of a true netherworld than the one I first found myself in," he said.

"I think you could be close to the truth," Hawkmoon told him as he bent to inspect the lock. Like so many of the other artefacts here it was crude. He took out the emerald-pommelled poignard which he had got off the mantis-warrior. He inserted the point in the lock and shifted it about for several seconds before twisting it sharply. There was a click and the door swung open.

The two companions stepped through.

And both gasped in unison at what they saw.

chapter two

A MUSEUM OF THE LIVING AND THE DEAD

"King Huon!" Hawkmoon murmured. Quickly he closed
the door behind him, looking up at the great globe suspended
above his head. In the globe swam the wizened figure of
the ancient king who had once spoken with the voice of a
golden youth. "I thought you slain by Meliadus!"

A tiny whisper escaped the globe. It was almost a thought,
so tenuous was it. "Meliadus," it said. "Meliadus."

"The king dreams," said the voice of Flana, Queen of
Granbretan.

And there she was, in her heron-mask, made up of frag-
ments of a thousand jewels, in her lush brocade gown,
coming slowly towards them.

"Flana?"

Hawkmoon moved towards her. "How did you come to
be here?"

"I was born in Londra. Who are you? Though you be of

the King-Emperor's own Order, you speak insolently to Flana, Countess of Kanbery."

"Queen Flana now," said Hawkmoon.

"Queen . . . queen . . . queen . . ." said the distant voice of King Huon from behind them.

"King . . ." Another figure moved blindly past them. "King Meliadus . . ."

And Hawkmoon knew that if he tore off that wolf-helm from the figure he would see the face of Baron Meliadus, his old foe. And he knew that the eyes would be glazed, as Flana's eyes would be glazed. There were others in this room—all Dark Empire folk. Flana's old husband, Asrovak Mikosevaar; Shenegar Trott in his silver mask; Pra Flenn, Duke of Lakasdeh, in his grinning dragon-helm, who had died before his nineteenth birthday and had personally slain over a hundred men and women before his eighteenth. Yet, for all that this was an assembly of the fiercest of the Granbretanian warlords, none attacked. They hardly lived at all. Only Flana—who still lived in Hawkmoon's world—seemed to be able to frame a coherent sentence. The rest were like sleep-walkers, mumbling one or two words, but no more. And Hawkmoon's and Count Brass's entrance into this weird museum of the living and the dead had set them to babbling, like birds in an aviary.

It was unnerving, particularly to Dorian Hawkmoon, who had slain many of these people himself. He seized upon Flana, ripping off his own mask so that she could see his face.

"Flana! Do you not recognise me? Hawkmoon? How came you here?"

"Remove your hand from me, warrior!" she said automatically, though it was plain she did not really care. Flana had never understood much concerning protocol. "I do not know you. Put your mask back on!"

"Then you, too, must have been drawn from a time before

we met—or else from some other world altogether," Hawk-moon said.

"Meliadus...Meliadus..." said the whispering voice of King Huon in the Throne Globe above their heads.

"King...king..." said wolf-masked Meliadus.

And: "The Runestaff..." murmured fat Shenegar Trott, who had died trying to possess that mystic wand..."The Runestaff..."

It was all they could speak of—their fears or their ambitions. The chief fears or ambitions which had driven them through their lives and brought about their ruin.

"You are right," said Hawkmoon to Count Brass. "This is the world of the dead. But who keeps these poor creatures here? For what purposes have they been resurrected? It is like an obscene treasure-house—human loot—the loot of time—all crowded together!"

"Aye," sniffed Count Brass. "I wonder if, until recently, I was part of this collection. Could that not be possible, Dorian Hawkmoon?"

"These are all Dark Empire folk," said Hawkmoon. "No, I think you were seized from a time before all these died. Your youth speaks for that—and your own recollection of the Battle of Tarkia."

"I thank you for that reassurance," said Count Brass.

Hawkmoon put a finger to his lips. "Do you hear something? In the passage?"

"Aye."

"Into the shadows," said Hawkmoon. "I think someone approaches. They might notice the guard gone."

Not one of the people in the room, even Flana, tried to stop them as they squeezed through the company and hid in the darkest corner, sheltered by the bulk of Adaz Promp and Jherek Nankenseen, who had ever enjoyed each other's company, even in life.

The door opened and there was Baron Kalan of Vitall,

Grand Master of the Order of the Serpent, all rage and bewilderment.

"The door open and the guards gone!" he raved. He glared at the company of living-dead. "Which of you did this? Is there one who does more than dream—who plots to rob me of my power? Who seeks that power for himself? You, Meliadus—do you wake?" He pulled the wolf-helm free, but Meliadus's face was blank.

Kalan slapped the face, but Meliadus did not react. He grunted.

"You, Huon? Even you are no longer as powerful as am I? Do you resent that?"

But Huon merely whispered the name of the one who would kill him. "Meliadus..." he whispered. "Meliadus..."

"Shenegar Trott? You, cunning one?" Kalan shook the unresponsive shoulder of the Count of Sussex. "Did you unlock the door and dismiss the guards. And why?" He frowned. "No, it could only be Flana..." He searched for the heron mask of Flana Mikosévaar, Countess of Kanbery, among those many masks (whose workmanship was noticeably superior to Kalan's). "Flana is the only one who suspects..."

"What do you want with me now, Baron Kalan?" said Flana, drifting forward. "I am tired. You must not disturb me."

"You cannot deceive me, traitress-to-be. If I have an enemy here, it is you. Who else could it be? It is in everyone's interest, save yours, for the old Empire to be restored."

"As usual, I fail to understand you, Kalan."

"Aye, it's true that you *should* not understand—but I wonder..."

"Your guards came in here," Flana went on. "They were impolite fellows, but one was handsome enough."

"Handsome? They removed their masks?"

"One did, aye."

Kalan's eyes darted this way and that as he considered the implications of her remark. "How...?" he muttered. "How...?" He looked hard at Flana. "I still think this is your doing!"

"I do not know of what you accuse me, Kalan, and I do not care, for this nightmare will end soon, as nightmares must."

Kalan's eyes glinted sardonically in his snake mask. "Think you, Madam?" He turned away to inspect the lock. "My plans go constantly awry. Every action I take leads to further complications. There must be a single action which will wipe out the complexities at a stroke. Oh, Hawkmoon, Hawkmoon, I wish you would die."

At this Hawkmoon stepped out swiftly and tapped Kalan upon the shoulder with the flat of his sword. Kalan turned and the tip of the sword slipped under the mask and rested against the throat.

"If the request had been couched more politely, in the first place," Hawkmoon said with grim humour, "I might have complied. But now you have offended me, Baron Kalan. Too often have you shown yourself unfriendly to me."

"Hawkmoon..." Kalan's voice sounded like those of the living-dead around him. "Hawkmoon..." He took a deep breath. "How did you come here?"

"Don't you know, Kalan?" Count Brass emerged, drawing off his own mask. He was grinning a big, wide grin—the first Hawkmoon had seen on his face since they had met in the Kamarg.

"Is this a counterplot—did *he* bring you——? No...He would not betray me. We have too much at stake."

"Who is that?"

But Kalan had become cautious. "Killing me at this point could easily bring disaster upon us all," he said.

"Aye—and not killing you, that could produce a similar effect!" Count Brass laughed. "Have we anything to lose, Baron Kalan?"

"You have your life to lose, Count Brass," Kalan said savagely. "At best you could become like these others. Is that an attractive thought?"

"No." Count Brass began to strip off the mantis-clothing which had covered his brass armour.

"Then do not be a fool!" Kalan hissed. "Kill Hawkmoon now!"

"What did you try to do, Kalan?" Hawkmoon interrupted. "Resurrect the whole Dark Empire? Did you hope to restore it here to its former glory—in a world where Count Brass and myself and the others never existed? But you found that when you went back into the past and brought them here to rebuild Londra, that their memories were poor. It was as if they all dreamed. They had too many conflicting experiences in their minds and this confused them—made their brains dormant. They could not remember details—that is why all your murals and your artefacts are so crude, is it not? Why your guards are so ineffectual, why they do not fight. And when they are killed here, they vanish—for even you cannot control time to the extent that it tolerates the paradox of the twice-dead. You began to realise that if you altered history—even if you were successful in re-establishing the Dark Empire—all would suffer from this mental confusion. Everything would break down as swiftly as you built it. Any triumph you had would turn to ashes. You would rule over unreal creatures in an unreal world."

Kalan shrugged. "But we have taken steps to adjust matters. There are solutions, Hawkmoon. Perhaps our ambitions have become a little less grandiose, but the result could be much the same."

"What do you intend to do?" Count Brass growled.

Kalan gave a humourless laugh. "Ah, that now depends

on what you do to me. Surely you can see that? Already
there are eddies of confusion in the time-streams. One dimension becomes clogged with the constituents of another.
Originally my scheme was simply to get vengeance on
Hawkmoon by having him killed by one of his friends. I'll
admit I was foolish to think it could be so simple. And also,
instead of remaining in your dreamlike state, you began to
wake, to reason, to refuse to listen to what I told you. That
is not what should have happened and I do not know why."

"By bringing my friends out of a time before any of us
had met, you created an entirely new stream of possibilities," said Hawkmoon. "And from these sprang dozens
more—half-worlds which you can't control, which become
confused with the one from which we all originally came..."

"Aye." Kalan nodded his great mask. "But there is still
hope, if you, Count Brass, slay this Hawkmoon. Surely you
realise that your friendship with him led directly to your
own death—or will lead to it in your future..."

"So Oladahn and the others were merely returned to their
own time, believing themselves to have dreamed what happened here?" said Hawkmoon.

"Even that dream will fade," said Kalan. "They will
never know that I tried to help them save their own lives."

"And why do you not kill me, Kalan? You have had the
opportunity. Is it, as I suspect, that if you do, then the logic
resulting from such an action leads inexorably to your own
destruction?"

Kalan was silent. But his silence confirmed the truth of
what Hawkmoon had said.

"And only if I am killed by one of my already dead
friends will it be possible to remove my unwanted presence
from all those possible worlds you have explored, those
half-worlds your instruments have detected, where you hope
to restore the Dark Empire? Is that why you are so insistent
on Count Brass killing me? And do you intend, once he

had done that, to restore the Dark Empire, unchallenged, to its original world—with yourselves ruling behind these puppets of yours?" Hawkmoon spread his hand to indicate the living-dead. Even Queen Flana was quiescent now as her brain shut off the information which might easily turn it insane. "These shadows will appear to be the great warlords come back from the dead, to hold sway over Granbretan again. You will even have a new Queen Flana to renounce the throne in favour of this Shadow Huon."

"You are an intelligent young man, for a savage." A languid voice came from the doorway. Hawkmoon kept the tip of his sword against Kalan's throat as he looked towards the source of the voice.

A bizarre figure stood there, between two mantis-masked guards who bore flame-lances and looked anything but indecisive. There were, it now seemed, others in this world who were more than shadows. Hawkmoon recognised the figure, clad in a gigantic mask which was also a working clock and was, even as its wearer spoke, chiming the first eight bars of Sheneven's *Temporal Antipathies*, all of gilded and enamelled brass, with numerals of inlaid mother-of-pearl and hands of filigree silver, balanced by a golden pendulum in a box worn upon his chest.

"I thought you might be here, too, My Lord Taragorm," said Hawkmoon. He lowered his sword as the flame-lances nudged his midriff.

Taragorm of the Palace of Time voiced his golden laughter.

"Greetings, Duke Dorian. You will note, I hope, that these two guards are not of the company of the Dreaming Ones. These escaped with me at the Siege of Londra, when it became obvious to Kalan and myself that the battle was lost to us. Even then we could probe a little way into the future. My sad accident was arranged—an explosion produced to cause my apparent death. And Kalan's suicide, as you already know, was in reality the occasion of his first jump through the dimensions. We have worked so well together, since then. But there have been a few complications, as you've guessed."

Kalan moved forward and took the swords of Count Brass and Hawkmoon. Count Brass was scowling but seemed too astonished to resist at that moment. He had never seen Taragorm, Master of the Palace of Time, before.

Taragorm continued, his voice of full of amusement. "Now that you have been gracious enough to visit us, I hope those complications can be dispensed with, at long last. I had not hoped for such a stroke of luck! You were ever headstrong, Hawkmoon."

"And how will you achieve it—freeing yourselves of the complications you have created?" Hawkmoon folded his arms on his chest.

The clock face inclined itself slightly to one side, the pendulum beneath continued to swing, balanced as it was by complicated machinery, allowing for every movement of Taragorm's body.

"You will know when we return to Londra shortly. I speak, of course, of the true Londra, where we are soon expected, not this poor imitation. Kalan's idea, not mine."

"You supported me!" said Kalan in an aggrieved tone. "And it is I who take all the risks, travelling back and forth through a thousand dimensions . . ."

"Let us not have our guests think us petty, Baron Kalan," Taragorm chided. There had always been something of a rivalry between the two of them. He bowed slightly to Count Brass and Hawkmoon. "Please come with us while we make the final preparations for our journey back to our old home."

Hawkmoon stood his ground. "If we refuse?"

"You will be stranded here forever. You know we cannot, ourselves, kill you. You bank on that, do you? Well, alive in this place or dead in another, it's all much of a muchness, friend Hawkmoon. And now, please cover up your naked face. I know it might seem rude, but I am dreadfully old-fashioned about such things."

"I regret that, in this too, I must give offence," said Hawkmoon with a small bow. He let the guards lead him through the door. He saluted the dull-eyed Flana and the others, who had even stopped breathing, it seemed. "Farewell, sad shades. I hope I shall, at length, be the cause of your release."

"I hope so, also," said Taragorm. And the hands on the face of his mask moved a fraction and this bell began to strike the hour.

chapter three

COUNT BRASS CHOOSES TO LIVE

They were back in Baron Kalan's laboratory.

Hawkmoon considered the two guards who now had their swords. He could tell that Count Brass was also wondering whether it would be possible to rush the flame-lances.

Kalan was already in the white pyramid, making adjustments to the smaller pyramids which were suspended before him. Because he was still wearing his serpent-mask, he had greater difficulty in manipulating the objects and arranging them to his satisfaction. It seemed to Hawkmoon, as he watched, that somehow this scene symbolised a salient aspect of the Dark Empire culture.

For some reason Hawkmoon felt singularly calm as he considered his situation. Instinct told him to bide his time, that the crucial moment of action would come quite soon. And for this reason he relaxed his body and took no notice of the guards with their flame-lances, concentrating on what Kalan and Taragorm were saying.

"The pyramid is almost ready," Kalan told Taragorm. "But we must leave swiftly."

"Are we all to crowd into that thing?" Count Brass said, and he laughed. Hawkmoon realised that Count Brass, too, was biding his time.

"Aye," said Taragorm. "All."

And, as they watched, the pyramid began to expand until it was twice its size, then three times, then four and at last it filled the entire cleared space in the centre of the laboratory and suddenly Count Brass, Hawkmoon, Taragorm and the two mantis-masked guards were engulfed by the pyramid and stood within it while Kalan, suspended above their heads, continued to play with his odd controls.

"You see," said Taragorm. His voice was amused. "Kalan's talents always lay in his understanding of the nature of space. Whereas mine, of course, lie in my understanding of time. That is why together we can produce such whimsicalities as this pyramid!"

And now the pyramid was travelling again, shunting through the myriad dimensions of Earth. Once more Hawkmoon saw bizarre scenery and peculiar mirror-images of his own world and many of them were not the same as those he had witnessed on his journey to Kalan's and Taragorm's half-world.

And then it seemed they were in the darkness of limbo again. Beyond the flickering walls of the pyramid Hawkmoon could see nothing but solid blackness.

"We are there," said Kalan, and he turned a crystal control. The vessel began to shrink again, growing smaller and smaller until it could barely contain Kalan's body. The sides of the pyramid clouded and turned to the familiar brilliant white. Hanging in the blackness over their heads it seemed to provide no illumination beyond its immediate area. Hawkmoon could see nothing of his own body, let alone those of the others. He knew only that his feet stood upon smooth and solid ground and that his nostrils picked up a damp, stale smell. He stamped his foot upon the ground and the sound echoed and echoed. It seemed that they were in a cavern of some kind.

Now Kalan's voice boomed from the pyramid.

"The moment has come. The resurrection of our great Empire is at hand. We, who can bring life to the dead and death to the living, who have remained faithful to the old ways of Granbretan, who are pledged to restore her greatness and her domination over the whole world, bring the faithful ones the creature they most desire to see. Behold!"

And suddenly Hawkmoon was engulfed in light. The source was a mystery, but the light blinded him and made him cover his eyes. He cursed as he turned this way and that, trying to avoid it.

"See how he wriggles," said Kalan of Vitall. "See how he cringes, this, our arch-enemy!"

Hawkmoon forced himself to stand still and open his eyes to the terrible light.

A dreadful whispering was coming from all around him now, and a slithering, and a hissing. He peered about him, but could still see nothing beyond the light. The whispering grew to a murmur and the murmur to a muttering and the muttering to a roar and the roar became a single word, voiced by what must have been a thousand throats.

"Granbretan! Granbretan! Granbretan!"

And then there was silence.

"Enough of this!" came the voice of Count Brass. "Have done with—aah!"

And now Count Brass, too, was surrounded with the same strange radiance.

"And here is the other," said Kalan's voice. "Faithful, look upon him and hate him, for this is Count Brass. Without his help, Hawkmoon would never have been able to destroy that which we love. By treachery, by stealth, by cowardice, by begging the assistance of those more powerful than themselves, they thought they could destroy the Dark Empire. But the Dark Empire is not destroyed. She will grow stronger and greater still! Behold, Count Brass!"

And Hawkmoon saw the white light surrounding Count Brass grow a peculiar blue colour and Count Brass's armour of brass glowed blue, too, and Count Brass clapped his gauntleted hands to his helmeted head and he opened his mouth and let out a scream of pain.

"Stop!" cried Hawkmoon. "Why torture him?"

Lord Taragorm's voice came from near by, soft and pleased. "Surely you know why, Hawkmoon?"

And now brands flared and Hawkmoon saw that, indeed, they stood in a great cavern. And the five of them—Count Brass, Lord Taragorm, the two guards and himself—stood upon the top of a ziggurat raised in the centre of the cavern, while Baron Kalan in his pyramid hovered above their heads.

And below there were at least a thousand masked figures, travesties of beasts, with heads of Pig and Wolf and Bear and Vulture, swarming below and screaming out now as Count Brass screamed and fell to his knees, still surrounded by the awful blue flame.

And the leaping light of the brands showed murals and carvings and bas-reliefs which were, in the details of their obscenity, evidently of true Dark Empire workmanship. And Hawkmoon knew that they must be in Londra proper, probably in some cavern beneath a cavern, far below the foundations of the city.

He tried to reach Count Brass, but the light around his own body stopped him.

"Torture me!" cried Hawkmoon. "Leave Count Brass and torture me!"

And again came Taragorm's soft, sardonic voice. "But we *do* torture you, Hawkmoon, do we not?"

"Here is the one who brought us to the edge of annihilation!" came Kalan's voice from above. "Here is the one who, in his pride, thought he had destroyed us. But we shall destroy him. And with his destruction will come an end to all restraint upon us. We shall emerge, we shall conquer. The dead shall return and lead us—King Huon . . ."

"King Huon!" roared the masked crowd.

"Baron Meliadus!" cried Kalan.

"Baron Meliadus!" roared the crowd.

"Shenegar Trott, Count of Sussex!"

"Shenegar Trott!"

"And all the great heroes and demigods of Granbretan shall return!"

"All! All!"

"Aye—all shall return. And they shall have vengeance upon this world!"

"Vengeance!"

"The Beasts shall have vengeance!"

And again, quite suddenly, the crowd fell silent.

And again Count Brass screamed and tried to rise on his knees and beat at his body as the blue flame brought pain.

Hawkmoon saw that Count Brass was sweating, that his eyes burned as if with fever, that his lips writhed.

"Stop!" he cried. He tried to break through the light which held him, but again without success. "Stop!"

But now the beasts were laughing. Pigs giggled, dogs cackled, wolves barked and insects hissed. They laughed to see Count Brass in such pain and his friend in such helpless misery.

And Hawkmoon realised they were trapped in a ritual— a ritual which had been promised these mask-wearers in return for their loyalty to the unregenerate lords of the Dark Empire.

And what would the ritual lead to?

He began to guess.

* * *

Count Brass rolled upon the floor now, nearly falling over the edge of the ziggurat. And, every time he came close to the edge, something rolled him back to the centre. The blue flame ate at his nerves and his screams came louder and louder. He had lost all dignity, all identity, in that pain.

Hawkmoon wept as he begged Kalan and Taragorm to desist.

At last it stopped. Count Brass got shakily to his feet. The blue light faded to white and then the white light faded, too. Count Brass's face was taut. His lips were all bloody. His eyes had horror in them.

"Would you kill yourself, Hawkmoon, to end your friend's agony?" Taragorm's taunting voice came from beside the Duke of Köln. "Would you do that?"

"So that is the alternative. Did your prognosis show you that your cause would triumph if I slew myself?"

"It improves our chances. It would be best if Count Brass could be prevailed upon to kill you but, if he will not..." Taragorm shrugged. "This is the next best thing."

Hawkmoon looked towards Count Brass. For an instant their eyes met and he stared in yellow orbs that were full of agony. Hawkmoon nodded. "I will do it. But first you must release Count Brass."

"Your own death will release Count Brass," said Kalan from above. "Be sure of that."

"I do not trust you," Hawkmoon said.

The beasts below watched on with bated breath as they waited for their enemy to die.

"Will this be sufficient evidence of our faith?" The white light faded from around Hawkmoon, too. Taragorm took Hawkmoon's sword from the soldier who still held it. He handed it to Hawkmoon. "There. Now you can kill me or kill yourself. Only be assured that if you kill me, Count Brass's torture will continue. If you kill yourself, it will cease."

Hawkmoon licked his dry lips. He looked from Count Brass to Taragorm to Kalan and to the blood-hungry crowd. To kill himself for the pleasure of these degenerates was loathsome. And yet, it was the only way to save Count Brass. But what of the rest of the world? He was too dazed to think of anything more, to consider any further possibilities.

Slowly he shifted his sword in his hand until the pommel was upon the flagstones and the tip under his breastplate, resting against his flesh.

"You will still perish," Hawkmoon said. His smile was bitter as he contemplated the frightful crowd. "Whether I live or die. You will perish because of the rot that is in your souls. You perished before because you turned inward upon each other as a response to the great danger which threatened you. You squabbled, beast against beast, as we attacked Londra. Could we have succeeded without your help? I think not."

"Be silent!" Kalan cried from his pyramid. "Do what you have agreed to do, Hawkmoon, or Count Brass begins to dance again!"

But then Count Brass's voice, deep and huge and weary, came from behind Hawkmoon.

Count Brass said:

"No!"

"If Hawkmoon goes back on his word, Count Brass, then back comes flame and pain . . ." said Taragorm, as one might address a child.

"No," said Count Brass. "I'll suffer no more."

"You wish to kill yourself, too?"

"My life means very little at this moment. It was because of Hawkmoon that I have suffered so. If he is to die, at least give me the pleasure of despatching him! I'll do what you wanted me to do in the first place. I see now that I have bore many ordeals for the sake of one who is, indeed, my enemy. Aye—let me kill him. Then I shall die. And I shall have died avenged."

The pain had plainly turned Count Brass mad. His yellow eyes rolled. His lips twisted back to reveal ivory teeth. "I shall have died avenged!"

Taragorm was surprised. "This is more than I hoped for. Our faith in you, Count Brass, was justified, after all." Taragorm's voice was gleeful as he took the brass-hilted broadsword from the mantis-guard and handed it to Count Brass.

Count Brass took his sword in both his great hands. His eyes narrowed as he turned to look at Hawkmoon.

"I shall feel better, taking an enemy with me," said Count Brass.

And he raised the long sword above his head. And his brass armour picked up the light from the brands and made his whole head and his whole body shine as if with fire.

And Hawkmoon peered into those yellow eyes and knew that he saw death there.

chapter four

A GREAT WIND BLOWING

But it was not his own death that Hawkmoon saw.

It was Taragorm's death.

In an instant Count Brass had shifted his stance, shouted to Hawkmoon to take the guards, and brought the massive sword down upon the ornate clock-mask.

There came a howl from below as the crowd understood what was happening. Beast-masks tossed from side to side as the Dark Empire creatures began to climb the steps of the ziggurat.

Kalan cried out from above. Hawkmoon, reversing his sword swiftly, swept it round to knock the flame-lances from the hands of the guards. They fell back. Kalan's voice continued to wail hysterically from the pyramid. "Fools! Fools!"

Taragorm was staggering. It was evidently Taragorm who controlled the white fire, for it flickered around Count

Brass as he raised his sword for a second blow. Taragorm's clock was split, the hands buckled, but the head beneath was evidently still intact.

The sword smashed into the ruined mask and the two sides fell away.

And there was revealed a head far smaller, in proportion, than the body on which it sat. A round, ugly head—the head of something which might have thrived during the Tragic Millennium.

And then that tiny, round, white thing was lopped from its stalk by a sideswipe of Count Brass's sword. Taragorm was now most certainly dead.

Beasts began to clamber onto the platform from all sides.

Count Brass roared with battle-joy as his sword took lives, as blood splashed in the flame-light, as men screamed and fell.

Hawkmoon was still engaged on the far side of the zig-gurat with the two mantis-guards who had drawn their own swords.

And now a great wind seemed to be blowing through the cavern, a whistling wind, a wailing wind.

Hawkmoon drove his sword point first through the eyeslit of the nearest mantis-warrior. He tugged the sword free and slashed at the other, driving the edge into the neck so hard that it smashed through the metal and severed the jugular. Now he could try to reach Count Brass.

"Count Brass!" he called. "Count Brass!"

Kalan was cackling in panic above. "The wind!" he cried. "The time-wind!"

But Hawkmoon ignored him. He was bent on reaching his friend's side and dying with his friend if need be.

But the wind blew still more strongly. It buffeted Hawk-moon. He found that he could barely move against it. And now breast-masked warriors of Granbretan were falling back, plunging over the sides of the ziggurat as the wind blew them, too.

Hawkmoon saw Count Brass swinging his broad-sword two-handed. The count's armour still shone like the sun itself. He had planted his feet upon a pile of those he had already slain and he was roaring with gigantic good humour as beasts came at him, slashing with swords and pikes and spears, his own blade moving with the regularity with which Taragorm's pendulum had once moved.

And Hawkmoon laughed, too. This would be the way to die, if die they must. Again he fought against the wind, wondering from where it came as he struggled to reach Count Brass.

But then he was picked up by it. He struggled as the ziggurat fell away below him and the scene became smaller and smaller, the figure of Count Brass himself so tiny that he could barely be seen now—and Kalan's white pyramid seemed to shatter as he passed it and Kalan screamed as he went tumbling down towards the fight.

Hawkmoon tried to see what held him. But nothing visible held him at all. Only the wind.

What had he heard Kalan call it? The time-wind?

Had they, then, in slaying Taragorm, released other forces of space and time—perhaps created the chaos which Kalan's and Taragorm's experiments had brought so close?

Chaos. Would he be blown forever upon this wind of time?

But no—he had left the cavern and was in Londra itself. Yet this was not the reformed Londra. This was the Londra of the old, bad days—the crazy towers and minarets, the jewelled domes, built upon both sides of the blood-red River Thayme. The wind had blown him into the past. Metal wings clashed as ornate ornithopters flew by. There seemed to be much activity in this Londra. For what did they prepare?

And again the scene shifted.

Again Hawkmoon looked down upon Londra. But now a battle raged. Explosions. Flame. The shouts of the dying. He recognised it. This was the Battle of Londra.

Down he began to tumble. Down and down until he could barely think and hardly knew who he was.

And then he was Dorian Hawkmoon, Duke von Köln, a flashing mirror-helm upon his head, the Sword of the Dawn in his hand, the Red Amulet about his throat and a Black Jewel embedded in his skull.

Again he was at the Battle of Londra.

And he thought his new thoughts and his old together as he spurred his horse into the fray. And there was a great pain in his head and he knew the Black Jewel gnawed at his brain.

All about him men were fighting. The strange Legion of the Dawn, emitting its rosy aura, was driving through warriors who wore fierce wolf and vulture helms. All was confusion. Through his pain-glazed eyes Hawkmoon could hardly see what was happening. He glimpsed one or two of his Kamargian warriors. He saw two or three other mirror-helms flashing in the thick of the battle. He realised that his own sword arm was rising and falling, rising and falling as he beat off the Dark Empire warriors who were on all sides of him.

"Count Brass," he murmured. "Count Brass." He remembered that he sought to be at the side of his old friend, though he hardly knew why. He saw the barbaric Warriors of the Dawn, with their painted bodies, their spiked clubs and their barbed lances decorated with tufts of dyed hair, slicing through the massed ranks of the Dark Empire warriors. He looked about him, trying to see which of those who wore the mirror-helms was Count Brass.

And still the pain in his skull grew and grew. And he gasped and wished that he could tear the mirror-helm free from his own head. But his hands were already occupied with fending off those warriors who pressed about him.

And then he saw something flash like gold and he knew it was the brazen hilt of Count Brass's sword and he spurred his horse through the throng.

The man in the mirror-helm and the armour of brass was fighting three great Dark Empire lords. Hawkmoon saw him standing there in the mud, horseless and brave, while the three—Hound, Goat and Bull—rode down on him. He saw Count Brass swing his broad-sword and cut at the legs of his opponents' horses so that Adaz Promp was thrown forward to land at Count Brass's feet and be swiftly slain. He saw Mygel Holst trying to get his feet, his arms widespread as he begged for mercy. He saw Mygel Holst's head fly from its shoulders. Now only one of the lords remained alive, Saka Gerden in his massive bull-helm, rising to his feet and shaking his head as the mirror-mask blinded him.

Hawkmoon ploughed on, still crying out: "Count Brass! Count Brass!"

Though he knew this was a dream, a distorted memory of the Battle of Londra, he still felt that he must reach his old friend's side. But before he could reach Count Brass, he saw the count wrench off his mirror-mask and face Saka Gerden bareheaded. Then the two closed.

Hawkmoon was nearly there by now, fighting wildly with his only object being to reach Count Brass.

And then Hawkmoon saw a rider of the Order of the Goat, a spear poised in his hand, riding down on Count Brass from behind. Hawkmoon yelled, spurred his horse forward and drove the Sword of the Dawn deep into the throat of the Goat rider just as Count Brass split the skull of Saka Gerden.

Hawkmoon kicked the corpse of the Goat Rider free from its saddle and called:

"A horse for you, Count Brass."

Count Brass offered Hawkmoon a quick grin of thanks and swung up into the saddle, his mirror-helm forgotten on the ground.

"Thanks!" shouted Count Brass above the din of the battle. "Now we'd best try to re-group our forces for the final assault."

His voice had a peculiar echo to it. Hawkmoon swayed in his saddle as the pain from the Black Jewel grew still more intense. He tried to reply, but he could not. He looked for Yisselda in the ranks of his own forces, but could not see her.

The horse seemed to gallop faster and faster as the battle-noise began to fade. Then he was no longer astride a horse at all. A wind blew him on. A strong, cold wind, like the wind that blew across the Kamarg.

The sky was darkening. The battle was behind him. He began to fall through the night. He saw swaying reeds where he had seen fighting men. He saw glistening lagoons and marshes. He heard the lonely bark of a marsh fox and he mistook it for Count Brass's voice.

And suddenly the wind no longer blew.

He tried to move of his own accord, but something tugged at his body. He no longer wore the mirror-helm. His sword was no longer in his hand. His vision cleared as the terrible pain fled from his skull.

He lay immersed in marsh mud. It was night-time. He was sinking slowly into the greedy earth. He saw part of the body of a horse just in front of him. He reached towards it, but only one arm was free from the mud now. He heard his name being called and he mistook it for the cry of a bird.

"Yisselda," he murmured. "Oh, Yisselda!"

chapter five

SOMETHING OF A DREAM

He felt as if he had already died. Fantasies and memories became confused as he waited for the marsh to swallow him. Faces appeared before him. He saw the face of Count Brass which shifted from relative youth to relative age even as he watched. He saw the face of Oladahn of the Bulgar Mountains. He saw Bowgentle and he saw D'Averc. He saw Yisselda. He saw Kalan of Vitall and Taragorm of the Palace of Time. Beast faces loomed on all sides. He saw Rinal of the Wraith-folk, Orland Fank of the Runestaff and his brother The Warrior in Jet and Gold. He saw Yisselda again. But weren't there other faces, too? Children's faces. Why did he not see them. And why did he confuse them with the face of Count Brass? Count Brass as a child? He had not known him then. He had not been born then.

Count Brass's face was concerned. It opened its lips. It spoke.

"Is that you, young Hawkmoon?"

"Aye, Count Brass. It is Hawkmoon. Shall we die to-gether?"

He smiled at the vision.

"He still raves," said a sad voice which was not that of Count Brass. "I am sorry, my lord. I should have tried to stop him."

Hawkmoon recognised the voice of Captain Josef Vedla.

"Captain Vedla? Have you come to pull me from the marsh for a second time?"

A rope fell near Hawkmoon's free hand. Automatically he passed his wrist through the loop. Someone began to pull at the rope. Slowly he was tugged free of the marsh.

His head was still aching, as if the Black Jewel had never been removed. But the ache was fading now and his brain was clearing. Why should he be reliving what was, after all, a fairly mundane incident in his life?—though he had come very close to death.

"Yisselda?" He looked for her face among those bending over him. But his fantasy remained. He still saw Count Brass, surrounded by his old Kamargian soldiers. There was no woman here at all.

"Yisselda?" he said again.

Count Brass said softly. "Come, lad, we'll take you back to Castle Brass."

Hawkmoon felt himself lifted in the count's massive arms and carried to a waiting horse.

"Can you ride yourself?" Count Brass asked.

"Aye." Hawkmoon clambered into the saddle of the horned stallion and straightened his back, swaying slightly as his feet sought the stirrups. He smiled. "Are you a ghost still, Count Brass? Or have you truly been restored to life. I said I would give anything for you to be brought back to us."

"Restored to life? You should know that I am not dead!"

Count Brass laughed. "And these fresh terrors come to haunt you, Hawkmoon?"

"You did not die at Londra?"

"Thanks to you, aye. You saved my life. If that Goat rider had got his spear into me, the chances are I'd be dead now."

Hawkmoon smiled to himself. "So events can be changed. And without repercussion, it seems. But where are Kalan and Taragorm now? And the others..." He turned to Count Brass as they rode together along the familiar marsh trails. "And Bowgentle, and Oladahn, and D'Averc?"

Count Brass frowned. "Dead these five years. Do you not remember? Poor lad, we all suffered after the Battle of Londra." He cleared his throat. "We lost much in our service of the Runestaff. And you lost your sanity."

"My sanity?"

The lights of Aigues-Mortes were coming in sight. Hawkmoon could see the outline of Castle Brass on the hill.

Again Count Brass cleared his throat. Hawkmoon stared at him, "My sanity, Count Brass?"

"I should not have mentioned it. We'll soon be home." Count Brass would not meet his gaze.

They rode through the gates of the town and began to ascend the winding streets. Some of the soldiers rode their horses in other directions as they neared the castle, for they had quarters in the town itself.

"Good night to you!" called Captain Vedla.

Soon only Count Brass and Hawkmoon were left. They entered the courtyard of the castle and dismounted.

The hall of the castle looked little different from when Hawkmoon had last seen it. Yet it had an empty feel to it.

"Is Yisselda sleeping?" Hawkmoon asked.

"Aye," said Count Brass wearily. "Sleeping."

Hawkmoon looked down at his mud-caked clothes. He

no longer wore armour. "I'd best bathe and get to bed myself," he said. He looked hard at Count Brass and then he smiled. "I thought you slain, you know, at the Battle of Londra."

"Aye," said Count Brass in the same troubled voice. "I know. But now you know I'm no ghost, eh?"

"Just so!" Hawkmoon laughed with joy. "Kalan's schemes served us much better than they served him, eh?"

Count Brass frowned. "I suppose so," he said uncertainly, as if he was not sure what Hawkmoon meant.

"Yet he escaped," Hawkmoon went on. "We could have trouble from him again."

"Escaped? No. He committed suicide after taking that jewel from your head. That is what disturbed your brain so much."

Hawkmoon began to feel afraid.

"You remember nothing of our most recent adventures then?" He moved to where Count Brass warmed himself at the fire.

"Adventures? You mean the marsh? You rode off in a trance, mumbling something of having seen me out there. Velda saw you leave and came to warn me. That is why we went in search of you and just managed to find you before you died . . ."

Hawkmoon stared hard at Count Brass and then he turned away. Had he dreamed all the rest. Had he truly been mad?

"How long have I—have I been in this trance you mention, Count Brass?"

"Why, since Londra. You seemed rational enough for a little while after the jewel was removed. But then you began to speak of Yisselda as if she still lived. And there were other references to some you thought dead—such as myself. It is not surprising that you should have suffered such strain, for the jewel was . . ."

"Yisselda!" Hawkmoon cried out in sudden grief. "You say she is dead?"

"Aye—at the Battle of Londra, fighting as well as any other warrior—she went down . . ."

"But the children—the children . . ." Hawkmoon struggled to remember the names of his children. "What were they called? I cannot quite recall . . ."

Count Brass sighed a deep sigh and put his gauntleted hand on Hawkmoon's shoulder. "You spoke of children, too. But there were no children. How could there be?"

"No children."

Hawkmoon felt strangely empty. He strove to remind himself of something he had said quite recently. *"I would give anything if Count Brass could live again . . ."*

And now Count Brass lived again and his love, his beautiful Yisselda, his children, they were gone to limbo—they had never existed in all those five years since the Battle of Londra.

"You seem more rational," said Count Brass. "I had begun to hope that your brain was healing. Now, perhaps, it has healed."

"Healed?" The word was a mockery. Hawkmoon turned again to confront his old friend. "Have all in Castle Brass— in the whole Kamarg—thought me mad?"

"Madness might be too strong a word," said Count Brass gruffly. "You were in a kind of trance, as if you dreamed of events slightly different to those which were actually taking place . . . that is the best way I can describe it. If Bowgentle were here, perhaps he could have explained it better. Perhaps he could have helped you more than we could." The count in brass shook his heavy, red head. "I do not know, Hawkmoon."

"And now I am sane," said Hawkmoon bitterly.

"Aye, it seems so."

"Then perhaps my madness was preferable to this reality." Hawkmoon walked heavily towards the stairs. "Oh, this is so hard to bear."

Surely it could not all have been a graphic dream. Surely Yisselda had lived and the children had lived?

But already the memories were fading, as a dream fades. At the foot of the stairs he turned again to where Count Brass still stood, looking into the fire, his old head heavy and sad.

"We live—you and I? And our friends are dead. Your daughter is dead. You were right, Count Brass—much was lost at the Battle of Londra. Your grandchildren were lost, also."

"Aye," said Count Brass almost inaudibly. "The future was lost, you could say."

epilogue

Nearly seven years had passed since the great Battle of Londra, when the power of the Dark Empire had been broken. And much had taken place in those seven years. For five of them Dorian Hawkmoon, Duke of Köln, had suffered the tragedy of madness. Even now, two years since he had recovered, he was not the same man who had ridden so bravely on the Runestaff's business. He had become grim, withdrawn and lonely. Even his old friend, Count Brass, the only other survivor of the conflict, hardly knew him now.

"It is the loss of his companions—the loss of his Yisselda," whispered the sympathetic townspeople of the restored Aigues-Mortes. And they would pity Dorian Hawkmoon as he rode, alone, through the town and out of the gates and across the wide Kamarg, across the marshlands where the giant scarlet flamingoes wheeled and the white bulls galloped.

And Dorian Hawkmoon would ride to a small hill which rose from the middle of the marsh and he would dismount and lead his horse up to the top where stood the ruin of an ancient church, built before the onset of the Tragic Millennium.

And he would look out across the waving reeds and the rippling lagoons as the mistral keened and its melancholy voice would echo the misery in his eyes.

And he would try to recall a dream.

A dream of Yisselda and two children whose names he could not remember. Had they ever had names in his dream?

A foolish dream, of what might have been, if Yisselda had survived the Battle of Londra.

And sometimes, when the sun began to set across the broad marshlands and the rain began to fall, perhaps, into the lagoons, he would stand upon the highest part of the ruin and raise his arms out to the ragged clouds which raced across the darkening sky and call her name into the wind.

"Yisselda! Yisselda!"

And his cry would be taken up by the birds which sailed upon that wind.

"Yisselda!"

And later Hawkmoon would lower his head and he would weep and he would wonder why he still felt, in spite of all the evident truth, that he might one day find his lost love again.

Why did he wonder if there were still some place—some other Earth perhaps—where the dead still lived? Surely such an obsession showed that there was a trace of madness left in his skull?

Then he would sigh and arrange his features so that none

who saw him would know that he had mourned and he would climb upon his horse and, as the dusk fell, ride back to Castle Brass where his old friend waited for him.

Where Count Brass waited for him.

This ends the first of the Chronicles of Castle Brass.

Stories

❖ of ❖

Swords and Sorcery